Aldous Huxley was bouxley
(the biographer and ed   dson
of Thomas Henry Huxl   was
fourteen, was the niece   was
his brother.

In 1916 Aldous Huxl   ...or College,
Oxford, despite a condition or near-blindness which had developed
while he was at Eton. During 1919 he married Maria Nys, a
Belgian, and in the same year he joined *The Athenaeum* under
Middleton Murry, Katherine Mansfield's husband. His first book
of verse had been published in 1916 and two more followed. Then,
in 1920, *Limbo*, a collection of short stories, was published. A year
later *Crome Yellow*, Huxley's first novel, appeared and his reputation
was firmly established. From the first, the public recognized that
the strength of Huxley's writing lay in his combination of dazzling
dialogue and surface cynicism (often very funny indeed) with a
foundation of great conviction in the emancipating influences he
was to exert.

For most of the 1920s Huxley lived in Italy, but in the 30s moved
to Sanary, near Toulon, where he wrote *Brave New World*. During
this decade he was deeply concerned with the Peace Pledge Union
but left Europe in 1937 as he believed the Californian climate
would help his eyesight, a constant burden. It was in California
that he became convinced of the value of mystical experience and
he described the effects of some of his experiments in this area in
Doors of Perception and *Heaven and Hell*.

Maria Nys Huxley died in 1955 and a year later Aldous married
Laura Archera, a concert violinist who had become a practising
psycho-therapist. They continued to live in California, where
Aldous Huxley died, in 1963.

By the same author

Novels
Point Counter Point
Antic Hay
Those Barren Leaves
Brave New World
Eyeless in Gaza
After Many a Summer
Ape and Essence
Time Must have a Stop
The Genius and the Goddess
Island

Short Stories
Limbo
Mortal Coils
Little Mexican
Two or Three Graces
Brief Candles
Collected Short Stories

Biography
Grey Eminence
The Devils of Loudun

Essays and Belles Lettres
On the Margin
Along the Road
Proper Studies
Do What You Will
Music at Night & Vulgarity in Literature
Texts and Pretexts (Anthology)
The Olive Tree
Ends and Means
The Art of Seeing
The Perennial Philosophy
Science, Liberty and Peace
Themes and Variations
The Doors of Perception
Heaven and Hell
Adonis and the Alphabet
Brave New World Revisited
Literature and Science
Collected Essays
The Human Situation (ed. Piero Ferrucci)
Mocksha

Travel
Jesting Pilate
Beyond the Mexique Bay

Poetry and Drama
Verses and a Comedy
The Gioconda Smile

For Children
The Crows of Pearblossom

ALDOUS HUXLEY

Crome Yellow

A TRIAD PANTHER BOOK

GRANADA PUBLISHING
London Toronto Sydney New York

Published by Granada Publishing Limited in 1977
Reprinted 1978, 1979, 1982

ISBN 0 586 04436 1

First published by Chatto & Windus Ltd 1921
Copyright © Mrs Laura Huxley 1921

Granada Publishing Limited
Frogmore, St Albans, Herts AL2 2NF
and
36 Golden Square, London W1R 4AH
515 Madison Avenue, New York, NY 10022, USA
117 York Street, Sydney, NSW 2000, Australia
100 Skyway Avenue, Rexdale, Ontario, M9W 3A6, Canada
61 Beach Road, Auckland, New Zealand

Printed and bound in Great Britain by
Hazell Watson & Viney Ltd
Aylesbury, Bucks
Set in Intertype Baskerville

Granada®
Granada Publishing®

CHAPTER I

Along this particular stretch of line no express had ever passed. All the trains – the few that there were – stopped at all the stations. Denis knew the names of those stations by heart. Bole, Tritton, Spavin Delawarr, Knipswich for Timpany, West Bowlby, and, finally, Camlet-on-the-Water. Camlet was where he always got out, leaving the train to creep indolently onward, goodness only knew whither, into the green heart of England.

They were snorting out of West Bowlby now. It was the next station, thank Heaven. Denis took his chattels off the rack and piled them neatly in the corner opposite his own. A futile proceeding. But one must have something to do. When he had finished, he sank back into his seat and closed his eyes. It was extremely hot.

Oh, this journey! It was two hours cut clean out of his life; two hours in which he might have done so much, so much – written the perfect poem, for example, or read the one illuminating book. Instead of which – his gorge rose at the smell of the dusty cushions against which he was leaning.

Two hours. One hundred and twenty minutes. Anything might be done in that time. Anything. Nothing. Oh, he had had hundreds of hours, and what had he done with them? Wasted them, spilt the precious minutes as though his reservoir were inexhaustible. Denis groaned in the spirit, condemned himself utterly with all his works. What right had he to sit in the sunshine, to occupy corner seats in third-class carriages, to be alive? None, none, none.

Misery and a nameless nostalgic distress possessed him. He was twenty-three, and oh! so agonizingly conscious of the fact.

The train came bumpingly to a halt. Here was Camlet at last. Denis jumped up, crammed his hat over his eyes, deranged his pile of baggage, leaned out of the window and shouted for a porter, seized a bag in either hand, and had to put them down again in order to open the door. When at last he had safely bundled himself and his baggage on to the platform, he ran up the train towards the van.

'A bicycle, a bicycle!' he said breathlessly to the guard. He felt himself a man of action. The guard paid no attention, but continued methodically to hand out, one by one, the packages labelled to Camlet. 'A bicycle!' Denis repeated. 'A green machine, cross-framed, name of Stone. S-T-O-N-E.'

'All in good time, sir,' said the guard soothingly. He was a large, stately man with a naval beard. One pictured him at home, drinking tea, surrounded by a numerous family. It was in that tone that he must have spoken to his children when they were tiresome. 'All in good time, sir.' Denis's man of action collapsed, punctured.

He left his luggage to be called for later, and pushed off on his bicycle. He always took his bicycle when he went into the country. It was part of the theory of exercise. One day one would get up at six o'clock and pedal away to Kenilworth, or Stratford-on-Avon – anywhere. And within a radius of twenty miles there were always Norman churches and Tudor mansions to be seen in the course of an afternoon's excursion. Somehow they never did get seen, but all the same it was nice to feel that the bicycle was there, and that one fine morning one really might get up at six.

Once at the top of the long hill which led up from Camlet station, he felt his spirits mounting. The world, he found, was good. The far-away blue hills, the harvests whitening on the slopes of the ridge along which his road led him, the tree-less sky-lines that changed as he moved – yes, they were all good. He was overcome by the beauty of those deeply em-bayed combes, scooped in the flanks of the ridge beneath him. Curves, curves : he repeated the word slowly, trying as he did so to find some term in which to give expression to his appreciation. Curves – no, that was inadequate. He made a gesture with his hand, as though to scoop the achieved expression out of the air, and almost fell off his bicycle. What was the word to describe the curves of those little valleys? They were as fine as the lines of a human body, they were informed with the subtlety of art. . . .

Galbe. That was a good word; but it was French. *Le galbe évasé de ses hanches* : had one ever read a French novel in which that phrase didn't occur? Some day he would compile a dictionary for the use of novelists. *Galbe, gonflé, goulu: parfum, peau, pervers, potelé, pudeur: vertu, volupté.*

But he really must find that word. Curves, curves. . . . Those little valleys had the lines of a cup moulded round a woman's breast; they seemed the dinted imprints of some huge divine body that had rested on these hills. Cumbrous locutions, these; but through them he seemed to be getting nearer to what he wanted. Dinted, dimpled, wimpled – his mind wandered down echoing corridors of assonance and alliteration ever further and further from the point. He was enamoured with the beauty of words.

Becoming once more aware of the outer world, he found himself on the crest of a descent. The road plunged down, steep and straight, into a considerable valley. There, on the opposite slope, a little higher up the valley, stood Crome, his destination. He put on his brakes; this view of Crome was pleasant to linger over. The façade with its three projecting towers rose precipitously from among the dark trees of the garden. The house basked in full sunlight; the old brick rosily glowed. How ripe and rich it was, how superbly mellow! And at the same time, how austere! The hill was becoming steeper and steeper; he was gaining speed in spite of his brakes. He loosed his grip of the levers, and in a moment was rushing headlong down. Five minutes later he was passing through the gate of the great courtyard. The front door stood hospitably open. He left his bicycle leaning against the wall and walked in. He would take them by surprise.

CHAPTER II

He took nobody by surprise; there was nobody to take. All was quiet; Denis wandered from room to empty room, looking with pleasure at the familiar pictures and furniture, at all the little untidy signs of life that lay scattered here and there. He was rather glad that they were all out; it was amusing to wander through the house as though one were exploring a dead, deserted Pompeii. What sort of life would the excavator reconstruct from these remains; how would he people these empty chambers? There was the long gallery, with its rows of respectable and (though, of course, one couldn't publicly admit it) rather boring Italian primitives, its Chinese sculptures, its unobtrusive, dateless furniture. There was the panelled drawing-room, where the huge chintz-covered arm-chairs stood, oases of comfort among the austere flesh-mortifying antiques. There was the morning-room, with its pale lemon walls, its painted Venetian chairs and rococo tables, its mirrors, its modern pictures. There was the library, cool, spacious, and dark, book-lined from floor to ceiling, rich in portentous folios. There was the dining-room, solidly, portwinily English, with its great mahogany table, its eighteenth-century chairs and sideboard, its eighteenth-century pictures – family portraits, meticulous animal paintings. What could one reconstruct from such data? There was much of Henry Wimbush in the long gallery and the library, something of Anne, perhaps, in the morning-room. That was all. Among the accumulations of ten generations the living had left but few traces.

Lying on the table in the morning-room he saw his own book of poems. What tact! He picked it up and opened it. It was what the reviewers call 'a slim volume.' He read at hazard :

> '. . . But silence and the topless dark
> Vault in the lights of Luna Park
> And Blackpool from the nightly gloom
> Hollows a bright tumultuous tomb.'

He put it down again, shook his head, and sighed. 'What genius I had then!' he reflected, echoing the aged Swift. It was nearly six months since the book had been published; he was glad to think he would never write anything of the same sort again. Who could have been reading it, he wondered? Anne, perhaps; he liked to think so. Perhaps, too, she had at last recognized herself in the Hamadryad of the poplar sapling; the slim Hamadryad whose movements were like the swaying of a young tree in the wind. 'The Woman who was a Tree' was what he had called the poem. He had given her the book when it came out, hoping that the poem would tell her what he hadn't dared to say. She had never referred to it.

He shut his eyes and saw a vision of her in a red velvet cloak, swaying into the little restaurant where they sometimes dined together in London – three quarters of an hour late, and he at his table, haggard with anxiety, irritation, hunger. Oh, she was damnable!

It occurred to him that perhaps his hostess might be in her boudoir. It was a possibility; he would go and see. Mrs Wimbush's boudoir was in the central tower on the garden front. A little staircase corkscrewed up to it from the hall. Denis mounted, tapped at the door. 'Come in.' Ah, she was there; he had rather hoped she wouldn't be. He opened the door.

Priscilla Wimbush was lying on the sofa. A blotting-pad rested on her knees and she was thoughtfully sucking the end of a silver pencil.

'Hullo,' she said, looking up. 'I'd forgotten you were coming.'

'Well, here I am, I'm afraid,' said Denis deprecatingly. 'I'm awfully sorry.'

Mrs Wimbush laughed. Her voice, her laughter, were deep and masculine. Everything about her was manly. She had a large, square, middle-aged face, with a massive projecting nose and little greenish eyes, the whole surmounted by a lofty and elaborate coiffure of a curiously improbable shade of orange. Looking at her, Denis always thought of Wilkie Bard as the cantatrice.

'That's why I'm going to
Sing in op'ra, sing in op'ra,
Sing in op-pop-pop-pop-popera.'

Today she was wearing a purple silk dress with a high collar and a row of pearls. The costume, so richly dowagerish, so suggestive of the Royal Family, made her look more than ever like something on the Halls.

'What have you been doing all this time?' she asked.

'Well,' said Denis, and he hesitated, almost voluptuously. He had a tremendously amusing account of London and its doings all ripe and ready in his mind. It would be a pleasure to give it utterance. 'To begin with,' he said . . .

But he was too late. Mrs Wimbush's question had been what the grammarians call rhetorical; it asked for no answer. It was a little conversational flourish, a gambit in the polite game.

'You find me busy at my horoscopes,' she said, without even being aware that she had interrupted him.

A little pained, Denis decided to reserve his story for more receptive ears. He contented himself, by way of revenge, with saying 'Oh?' rather icily.

'Did I tell you how I won four hundred on the Grand National this year?'

'Yes,' he replied, still frigid and monosyllabic. She must have told him at least six times.

'Wonderful, isn't it? Everything is in the Stars. In the Old Days, before I had the Stars to help me, I used to lose thousands. Now' – she paused an instant – 'well, look at that four hundred on the Grand National. That's the Stars.'

Denis would have liked to hear more about the Old Days. But he was too discreet and, still more, too shy to ask. There had been something of a bust up; that was all he knew. Old Priscilla – not so old then, of course, and sprightlier – had lost a great deal of money, dropped it in handfuls and hatfuls on every racecourse in the country. She had gambled too. The number of thousands varied in the different legends, but all put it high. Henry Wimbush was forced to sell some of his Primitives – a Taddeo da Poggibonsi, an Amico di Taddeo, and four or five nameless Sienese – to the Americans. There was a crisis. For the first time in his life Henry asserted himself, and with good effect, it seemed.

Priscilla's gay and gadding existence had come to an abrupt end. Nowadays she spent almost all her time at Crome, cultivating a rather ill-defined malady. For consolation she dallied with New Thought and the Occult. Her passion for racing still possessed her, and Henry, who was a kind-hearted fellow at bottom, allowed her forty pounds a month betting money. Most of Priscilla's days were spent in casting the horoscopes of horses, and she invested her money scientifically, as the Stars dictated. She betted on football too, and had a large notebook in which she registered the horoscopes of all the players in all the teams of the League. The process of balancing the horoscopes of two elevens one against the other was a very delicate and difficult one. A match between the Spurs and the Villa entailed a conflict in the heavens so vast and so complicated that it was not to be wondered at if she sometimes made a mistake about the outcome.

'Such a pity you don't believe in these things, Denis, such a pity,' said Mrs Wimbush in her deep, distinct voice.

'I can't say I feel it so.'

'Ah, that's because you don't know what it's like to have faith. You've no idea how amusing and exciting life becomes when you do believe. All that happens means something; nothing you do is ever insignificant. It makes life so jolly, you know. Here am I at Crome. Dull as ditchwater, you'd think; but no, I don't find it so. I don't regret the Old Days a bit. I have the Stars . . .' She picked up the sheet of paper that was lying on the blotting-pad. 'Inman's horoscope,' she explained. '(I thought I'd like to have a little fling on the billiards championship this autumn.) I have the Infinite to keep in tune with,' she waved her hand. 'And then there's the next world and all the spirits, and one's Aura, and Mrs Eddy and saying you're not ill, and the Christian Mysteries and Mrs Besant. It's all splendid. One's never dull for a moment. I can't think how I used to get on before – in the Old Days. Pleasure? – running about, that's all it was; just running about. Lunch, tea, dinner, theatre, supper, every day. It was fun, of course, while it lasted. But there wasn't much left of it afterwards. There's rather a good thing about that in Barbecue-Smith's new book. Where is it?'

She sat up and reached for a book that was lying on the little table by the head of the sofa.

'Do you know him, by the way?' she asked.

'Who?'

11

'Mr Barbecue-Smith.'

Denis knew of him vaguely. Barbecue-Smith was a name in the Sunday papers. He wrote about the Conduct of Life. He might even be the author of *What a Young Girl Ought to Know*.

'No, not personally,' he said.

'I've invited him for next week-end.' She turned over the pages of the book. 'Here's the passage I was thinking of. I marked it. I always mark the things I like.'

Holding the book almost at arm's length, for she was somewhat long-sighted, and making suitable gestures with her free hand, she began to read, slowly, dramatically.

' "What are thousand pound fur coats, what are quarter million incomes?" ' She looked up from the page with a histrionic movement of the head; her orange coiffure nodded portentously. Denis looked at it, fascinated. Was it the Real Thing and henna, he wondered, or was it one of those Complete Transformations one sees in the advertisements?

' "What are Thrones and Sceptres?" '

The orange Transformation – yes, it must be a Transformation – bobbed up again.

' "What are the gaieties of the Rich, the splendours of the Powerful, what is the pride of the Great, what are the gaudy pleasures of High Society?" '

The voice, which had risen in tone, questioningly, from sentence to sentence, dropped suddenly and boomed reply.

' "They are nothing. Vanity, fluff, dandelion seed in the wind, thin vapours of fever. The things that matter happen in the heart. Seen things are sweet, but those unseen are a thousand times more significant. It is the Unseen that counts in Life." '

Mrs Wimbush lowered the book. 'Beautiful, isn't it?' she said.

Denis preferred not to hazard an opinion, but uttered a non-committal 'H'm.'

'Ah, it's a fine book this, a beautiful book,' said Priscilla, as she let the pages flick back, one by one, from under her thumb. 'And here's the passage about the Lotus Pool. He compares the Soul to a Lotus Pool, you know.' She held up the book again and read. ' "A Friend of mine has a Lotus Pool in his garden. It lies in a little dell embowered with wild roses and eglantine, among which the nightingale pours forth its amorous descant all the summer long. Within the pool the Lotuses blossom, and the birds of the air come to drink and bathe themselves in its crystal waters. . ." Ah, and that reminds me,' Priscilla exclaimed, shutting the book with a clap and uttering her big profound laugh – 'that reminds me of the things that have been going on in our bathing-pool since you were here last. We gave the village people leave to come and bathe here in the evenings. You've no idea of the things that happened.'

She leaned forward, speaking in a confidential whisper; every now and then she uttered a deep gurgle of laughter. '. . . mixed bathing . . . saw them out of my window . . . sent for a pair of field-glasses to make sure . . . no doubt of it. . . .' The laughter broke out again. Denis laughed too. Barbecue-Smith was tossed on the floor.

'It's time we went to see if tea's ready,' said Priscilla. She hoisted herself up from the sofa and went swishing off across the room, striding beneath the trailing silk. Denis followed her, faintly humming to himself :

> 'That's why I'm going to
> Sing in op'ra, sing in op'ra,
> Sing in op-pop-pop-pop-popera.'

And then the little twiddly bit of accompaniment at the end : 'ra-ra.'

CHAPTER III

The terrace in front of the house was a long narrow strip of turf, bounded along its outer edge by a graceful stone balustrade. Two little summer-houses of brick stood at either end. Below the house the ground sloped very steeply away, and the terrace was a remarkably high one; from the balusters to the sloping lawn beneath was a drop of thirty feet. Seen from below, the high unbroken terrace wall, built like the house itself of brick, had the almost menacing aspect of a fortification – a castle bastion, from whose parapet one looked out across airy depths to distances level with the eye. Below, in the foreground, hedged in by solid masses of sculptured yew trees, lay the stone-brimmed swimming-pool. Beyond it stretched the park, with its massive elms, its green expanses of grass, and, at the bottom of the valley, the gleam of the narrow river. On the farther side of the stream the land rose again in a long slope, chequered with cultivation. Looking up the valley, to the right, one saw a line of blue, far-off hills.

The tea-table had been planted in the shade of one of the little summer-houses, and the rest of the party was already assembled about it when Denis and Priscilla made their appearance. Henry Wimbush had begun to pour out the tea. He was one of those ageless, unchanging men on the farther side of fifty, who might be thirty, who might be anything. Denis had known him almost as long as he could remember. In all those years his pale, rather handsome face had never grown any older; it was like the pale grey bowler hat which he always wore, winter and summer – unageing, calm, serenely without expression.

Next him, but separated from him and from the rest of the world by the almost impenetrable barriers of her deafness, sat Jenny Mullion. She was perhaps thirty, had a tilted nose and a pink-and-white complexion, and wore her brown hair plaited and coiled in two lateral buns over her ears. In the secret tower of her deafness she sat apart, looking down at the world through sharply piercing eyes. What did she think of men and women and things? That was something that Denis had never been able to discover. In her enigmatic remoteness Jenny was a little disquieting. Even now some interior joke seemed to be amusing her, for she was smiling to herself, and her brown eyes were like very bright round marbles.

On his other side the serious, moon-like innocence of Mary Bracegirdle's face shone pink and childish. She was nearly twenty-three, but one wouldn't have guessed it. Her short hair, clipped like a page's, hung in a bell of elastic gold about her cheeks. She had large blue china eyes, whose expression was one of ingenuous and often puzzled earnestness.

Next to Mary a small gaunt man was sitting, rigid and erect in his chair. In appearance Mr Scogan was like one of those extinct bird-lizards of the Tertiary. His nose was beaked, his dark eye had the shining quickness of a robin's. But there was nothing soft or gracious or feathery about him. The skin of his wrinkled brown face had a dry and scaly look; his hands were the hands of a crocodile. His movements were marked by the lizard's disconcertingly abrupt clockwork speed; his speech was thin, fluty, and dry. Henry Wimbush's schoolfellow and exact contemporary, Mr Scogan looked far older and, at the same time, far more youthfully alive than did that gentle aristocrat with the face like a grey bowler.

Mr Scogan might look like an extinct saurian, but Gombauld was altogether and essentially human. In the old-fashioned natural histories of the 'thirties he might have figured in a steel engraving as a type of Homo Sapiens – an honour which at that time commonly fell to Lord Byron. Indeed, with more hair and less collar, Gombauld would have been completely Byronic – more than Byronic, even, for Gombauld was of Provençal descent, a black-haired young corsair of thirty, with flashing teeth and luminous large dark eyes. Denis looked at him enviously. He was jealous of his talent : if only he wrote verse as well as Gombauld painted pictures ! Still more, at the moment, he envied Gombauld his looks, his vitality, his easy confidence of manner. Was it surprising that Anne should like him? Like him? – it might even be something worse, Denis reflected bitterly, as he walked at Priscilla's side down the long grass terrace.

Between Gombauld and Mr Scogan a very much lowered deck-chair presented its back to the new arrivals as they advanced towards the tea-table. Gombauld was leaning over it;

his face moved vivaciously; he smiled, he laughed, he made quick gestures with his hands. From the depths of the chair came up a sound of soft, lazy laughter. Denis started as he heard it. That laughter – how well he knew it! What emotions it evoked in him! He quickened his pace.

In her low deck-chair Anne was nearer to lying than to sitting. Her long, slender body reposed in an attitude of listless and indolent grace. Within its setting of light brown hair her face had a pretty regularity that was almost doll-like. And indeed there were moments when she seemed nothing more than a doll; when the oval face, with its long-lashed, pale blue eyes, expressed nothing; when it was no more than a lazy mask of wax. She was Henry Wimbush's own niece; that bowler-like countenance was one of the Wimbush heirlooms; it ran in the family, appearing in its female members as a blank doll-face. But across this dollish mask, like a gay melody dancing over an unchanging fundamental bass, passed Anne's other inheritance – quick laughter, light ironic amusement, and the changing expressions of many moods. She was smiling now as Denis looked down at her : her cat's smile, he called it, for no very good reason. The mouth was compressed, and on either side of it two tiny wrinkles had formed themselves in her cheeks. An infinity of slightly malicious amusement lurked in those little folds, in the puckers about the half-closed eyes, in the eyes themselves, bright and laughing between the narrowed lids.

The preliminary greetings spoken, Denis found an empty chair between Gombauld and Jenny and sat down.

'How are you, Jenny?' he shouted at her.

Jenny nodded and smiled in mysterious silence, as though the subject of her health were a secret that could not be publicly divulged.

'How's London been since I went away?' Anne inquired from the depth of her chair.

The moment had come; the tremendously amusing narrative was waiting for utterance. 'Well,' said Denis, smiling happily, 'to begin with ...'

'Has Priscilla told you of our great antiquarian find?' Henry Wimbush leaned forward; the most promising of buds was nipped.

'To begin with,' said Denis desperately, 'there was the Ballet...'

'Last week,' Mr Wimbush went on softly and implacably, 'we dug up fifty yards of oaken drain-pipes; just tree trunks with a hole bored through the middle. Very interesting indeed. Whether they were laid down by the monks in the fifteenth century, or whether...'

Denis listened gloomily. 'Extraordinary!' he said, when Mr Wimbush had finished; 'quite extraordinary!' He helped himself to another slice of cake. He didn't even want to tell his tale about London now; he was damped.

For some time past Mary's grave blue eyes had been fixed upon him. 'What have you been writing lately?' she asked. It would be nice to have a little literary conversation.

'Oh, verse and prose,' said Denis – 'just verse and prose.'

'Prose?' Mr Scogan pounced alarmingly on the word. 'You've been writing prose?'

'Yes.'

'Not a novel?'

'Yes.'

'My poor Denis!' exclaimed Mr Scogan. 'What about?'

Denis felt rather uncomfortable. 'Oh, about the usual things, you know.'

'Of course,' Mr Scogan groaned. 'I'll describe the plot for you. Little Percy, the hero, was never good at games, but he was always clever. He passes through the usual public school and the usual university and comes to London, where he lives among the artists. He is bowed down with melancholy thought; he carries the whole weight of the universe upon his shoulders. He writes a novel of dazzling brilliance; he dabbles delicately in Amour and disappears, at the end of the book, into the luminous Future.'

Denis blushed scarlet. Mr Scogan had described the plan of his novel with an accuracy that was appalling. He made an effort to laugh. 'You're entirely wrong,' he said. 'My novel is not in the least like that.' It was a heroic lie. Luckily, he reflected, only two chapters were written. He would tear them up that very evening when he unpacked.

Mr Scogan paid no attention to his denial, but went on: 'Why will you young men continue to write about things that are so entirely uninteresting as the mentality of adolescents and artists? Professional anthropologists might find it interesting to turn sometimes from the beliefs of the Black-fellow to the philosophical preoccupations of the under-graduate. But you can't expect an ordinary adult man, like myself, to be much moved by the story of his spiritual troubles. And after all, even in England, even in Germany and Russia, there are more adults than adolescents. As for the artist, he is preoccupied with problems that are so utterly unlike those of the ordinary adult man – problems of pure aesthetics which don't so much as present themselves to people like myself – that a description of his mental pro-cesses is as boring to the ordinary reader as a piece of pure mathematics. A serious book about artists regarded as artists is unreadable; and a book about artists regarded as lovers, husbands, dipsomaniacs, heroes, and the like is really not worth writing again. Jean-Christophe is the stock artist of literature, just as Professor Radium of *Comic Cuts* is its stock man of science.'

'I'm sorry to hear I'm as uninteresting as all that,' said Gombauld.

'Not at all, my dear Gombauld,' Mr Scogan hastened to explain. 'As a lover or a dipsomaniac, I've no doubt of your being a most fascinating specimen. But as a combiner of forms, you must honestly admit it, you're a bore.'

'I entirely disagree with you,' exclaimed Mary. She was somehow always out of breath when she talked, and her speech was punctuated by little gasps. 'I've known a great many artists, and I've always found their mentality very interesting. Especially in Paris. Tschuplitski, for example – I saw a great deal of Tschuplitski in Paris this spring....'

'Ah, but then you're an exception, Mary, you're an ex-ception,' said Mr Scogan. 'You are a *femme supérieure*.'

A flush of pleasure turned Mary's face into a harvest moon.

CHAPTER IV

Denis woke up next morning to find the sun shining, the sky serene. He decided to wear white flannel trousers – white flannel trousers and a black jacket, with a silk shirt and his new peach-coloured tie. And what shoes? White was the obvious choice, but there was something rather pleasing about the notion of black patent leather. He lay in bed for several minutes considering the problem.

Before he went down – patent leather was his final choice – he looked at himself critically in the glass. His hair might have been more golden, he reflected. As it was, its yellowness had the hint of a greenish tinge in it. But his forehead was good. His forehead made up in height what his chin lacked in prominence. His nose might have been longer, but it would pass. His eyes might have been blue and not green. But his coat was very well cut and, discreetly padded, made him seem robuster than he actually was. His legs, in their white casing, were long and elegant. Satisfied, he descended the stairs. Most of the party had already finished their breakfast. He found himself alone with Jenny.

'I hope you slept well,' he said.

'Yes, isn't it lovely?' Jenny replied, giving two rapid little nods. 'But we had such awful thunderstorms last week.'

Parallel straight lines, Denis reflected, meet only at infinity. He might talk for ever of care-charmer sleep and she of meteorology till the end of time. Did one ever establish contact with anyone? We are all parallel straight lines. Jenny was only a little more parallel than most.

'They are very alarming, these thunderstorms,' he said, helping himself to porridge. 'Don't you think so? Or are you above being frightened?'

'No. I always go to bed in a storm. One is so much safer lying down.'

'Why?'

'Because,' said Jenny, making a descriptive gesture, 'because lightning goes downwards and not flat ways. When you're lying down you're out of the current.'

'That's very ingenious.'

'It's true.'

There was a silence. Denis finished his porridge and helped himself to bacon. For lack of anything better to say, and because Mr Scogan's absurd phrase was for some reason running in his head, he turned to Jenny and asked :

'Do you consider yourself a *femme supérieure*?' He had to repeat the question several times before Jenny got the hang of it.

'No,' she said rather indignantly, when at last she heard what Denis was saying. 'Certainly not. Has anyone been suggesting that I am?'

'No,' said Denis. 'Mr Scogan told Mary she was one.'

'Did he?' Jenny lowered her voice. 'Shall I tell you what I think of that man? I think he's slightly sinister.'

Having made this pronouncement, she entered the ivory tower of her deafness and closed the door. Denis could not induce her to say anything more, could not induce her even to listen. She just smiled at him, smiled and occasionally nodded.

Denis went out on to the terrace to smoke his after-breakfast pipe and to read his morning paper. An hour later, when Anne came down, she found him still reading. By this time he had got to the Court Circular and the Forthcoming Weddings. He got up to meet her as she approached, a Hamadryad in white muslin, across the grass.

'Why, Denis,' she exclaimed, 'you look perfectly sweet in your white trousers.'

Denis was dreadfully taken aback. There was no possible retort. 'You speak as though I were a child in a new frock,' he said, with a show of irritation.

'But that's how I feel about you, Denis dear.'

'Then you oughtn't to.'

'But I can't help it. I'm so much older than you.'

'I like that,' he said. 'Four years older.'

'And if you do look perfectly sweet in your white trousers, why shouldn't I say so? And why did you put them on, if you didn't think you were going to look sweet in them?'

'Let's go into the garden,' said Denis. He was put out; the conversation had taken such a preposterous and unexpected turn. He had planned a very different opening, in which he was to lead off with, 'You look adorable this morning,' or something of the kind, and she was to answer, 'Do I?' and then there was to be a pregnant silence. And now she had got in first with the trousers. It was provoking; his pride was hurt.

That part of the garden that sloped down from the foot of the terrace to the pool had a beauty which did not depend on colour so much as on forms. It was as beautiful by moonlight as in the sun. The silver of water, the dark shapes of yew and ilex trees remained, at all hours and seasons, the dominant features of the scene. It was a landscape in black and white. For colour there was the flower-garden; it lay to one side of the pool, separated from it by a huge Babylonian wall of yews. You passed through a tunnel in the hedge, you opened a wicket in a wall, and you found yourself, startlingly and suddenly, in the world of colour. The July borders blazed and flared under the sun. Within its high brick walls the garden was like a great tank of warmth and perfume and colour.

Denis held open the little iron gate for his companion. 'It's like passing from a cloister into an Oriental palace,' he said, and took a deep breath of the warm, flower-scented air. ' "In fragrant volleys they let fly . . ." How does it go?

> ' "Well shot, ye firemen ! O how sweet
> And round your equal fires do meet;
> Whose shrill report no ear can tell,
> But echoes to the eye and smell . . ." '

'You have a bad habit of quoting,' said Anne. 'As I never know the context or author, I find it humiliating.'

Denis apologized. 'It's the fault of one's education. Things somehow seem more real and vivid when one can apply somebody else's ready-made phrase about them. And then there are lots of lovely names and words – Monophysite, Iamblichus, Pomponazzi; you bring them out triumphantly, and feel you've clinched the argument with the mere magical sound of them. That's what comes of the higher education.'

'You may regret your education,' said Anne; 'I'm ashamed of my lack of it. Look at those sunflowers ! Aren't they magnificent?'

'Dark faces and golden crowns – they're kings in Ethiopia. And I like the way the tits cling to the flowers and pick out the seeds, while the other loutish birds, grubbing dirtily for their food, look up in envy from the ground. Do they look up in envy? That's the literary touch, I'm afraid. Education again. It always comes back to that.' He was silent.

Anne had sat down on a bench that stood in the shade of an old apple tree. 'I'm listening,' she said.

He did not sit down, but walked backwards and forwards in front of the bench, gesticulating a little as he talked. 'Books,' he said – 'books. One reads so many, and one sees so few people and so little of the world. Great thick books about the universe and the mind and ethics. You've no idea how many there are. I must have read twenty or thirty tons of them in the last five years. Twenty tons of ratiocination. Weighted with that, one's pushed out into the world.'

He went on walking up and down. His voice rose, fell, was silent a moment, and then talked on. He moved his hands, sometimes he waved his arms. Anne looked and listened quietly, as though she were at a lecture. He was a nice boy, and today he looked charming – charming!

One entered the world, Denis pursued, having ready-made ideas about everything. One had a philosophy and tried to make life fit into it. One should have lived first and then made one's philosophy to fit life. . . . Life, facts, things were horribly complicated; ideas, even the most difficult of them, deceptively simple. In the world of ideas everything was clear; in life all was obscure, embroiled. Was it surprising that one was miserable, horribly unhappy? Denis came to a halt in front of the bench, and as he asked this last question he stretched out his arms and stood for an instant in an attitude of crucifixion, then let them fall again to his sides.

'My poor Denis!' Anne was touched. He was really too pathetic as he stood there in front of her in his white flannel trousers. 'But does one suffer about these things? It seems very extraordinary.'

'You're like Scogan,' cried Denis bitterly. 'You regard me as a specimen for an anthropologist. Well, I suppose I am.'

'No, no,' she protested, and drew in her skirt with a gesture that indicated that he was to sit down beside her. He sat down. 'Why can't you just take things for granted and

22

as they come?' she asked. 'It's so much simpler.'

'Of course it is,' said Denis. 'But it's a lesson to be learnt gradually. There are the twenty tons of ratiocination to be got rid of first.'

'I've always taken things as they come,' said Anne. 'It seems so obvious. One enjoys the pleasant things, avoids the nasty ones. There's nothing more to be said.'

'Nothing – for you. But, then, you were born a pagan; I am trying laboriously to make myself one. I can take nothing for granted, I can enjoy nothing as it comes along. Beauty, pleasure, art, women – I have to invent an excuse, a justification for everything that's delightful. Otherwise I can't enjoy it with an easy conscience. I make up a little story about beauty and pretend that it has something to do with truth and goodness. I have to say that art is the process by which one reconstructs the divine reality out of chaos. Pleasure is one of the mystical roads to union with the in-finite – the ecstasies of drinking, dancing, love-making. As for women, I am perpetually assuring myself that they're the broad highway to divinity. And to think that I'm only just beginning to see through the silliness of the whole thing! It's incredible to me that anyone should have escaped these horrors.'

'It's still more incredible to me,' said Anne, 'that anyone should have been a victim to them. I should like to see myself believing that men are the highway to divinity.' The amused malice of her smile planted two little folds on either side of her mouth, and through their half-closed lids her eyes shone with laughter. 'What you need, Denis, is a nice plump young wife, a fixed income, and a little congenial but regular work.'

'What I need is you.' That was what he ought to have re-torted, that was what he wanted passionately to say. He could not say it. His desire fought against his shyness. 'What I need is you.' Mentally he shouted the words, but not a sound issued from his lips. He looked at her despairingly. Couldn't she see what was going on inside him? Couldn't she understand? 'What I need is you.' He would say it, he would – he would.

'I think I shall go and bathe,' said Anne. 'It's so hot.' The opportunity had passed.

CHAPTER V

Mr Wimbush had taken them to see the sights of the Home Farm, and now they were standing, all six of them – Henry Wimbush, Mr Scogan, Denis, Gombauld, Anne, and Mary – by the low wall of the piggery, looking into one of the styes.

'This is a good sow,' said Henry Wimbush. 'She had a litter of fourteen.'

'Fourteen?' Mary echoed incredulously. She turned astonished blue eyes towards Mr Wimbush, then let them fall on to the seething mass of *élan vital* that fermented in the sty.

An immense sow reposed on her side in the middle of the pen. Her round, black belly, fringed with a double line of dugs, presented itself to the assault of an army of small, brownish-black swine. With a frantic greed they tugged at their mother's flank. The old sow stirred sometimes uneasily or uttered a little grunt of pain. One small pig, the runt, the weakling of the litter, had been unable to secure a place at the banquet. Squealing shrilly, he ran backwards and forwards, trying to push in among his stronger brothers or even to climb over their tight little black backs towards the maternal reservoir.

'There *are* fourteen,' said Mary. 'You're quite right. I counted. It's extraordinary.'

'The sow next door,' Mr Wimbush went on, 'has done very badly. She only had five in her litter. I shall give her another chance. If she does no better next time, I shall fat her up and kill her. There's the boar,' he pointed towards a farther sty. 'Fine old beast, isn't he? But he's getting past his prime. He'll have to go too.'

'How cruel!' Anne exclaimed.

'But how practical, how eminently realistic!' said Mr Scogan. 'In this farm we have a model of sound paternal government. Make them breed, make them work, and when they're past working or breeding or begetting, slaughter them.'

'Farming seems to be mostly indecency and cruelty,' said Anne.

With the ferrule of his walking-stick Denis began to scratch the boar's long bristly back. The animal moved a little so as to bring himself within easier range of the instrument that evoked in him such delicious sensations; then he stood stock still, softly grunting his contentment. The mud of years flaked off his sides in a grey powdery scurf.

'What a pleasure it is,' said Denis, 'to do somebody a kindness. I believe I enjoy scratching this pig quite as much as he enjoys being scratched. If only one could always be kind with so little expense of trouble. . . .'

A gate slammed; there was a sound of heavy footsteps.

'Morning, Rowley!' said Henry Wimbush.

'Morning, sir,' old Rowley answered. He was the most venerable of the labourers on the farm – a tall, solid man, still unbent, with grey side-whiskers and a steep, dignified profile. Grave, weighty in his manner, splendidly respectable, Rowley had the air of a great English statesman of the mid-nineteenth century. He halted on the outskirts of the group, and for a moment they all looked at the pigs in a silence that was only broken by the sound of grunting or the squelch of a sharp hoof in the mire. Rowley turned at last, slowly and ponderously and nobly, as he did everything, and addressed himself to Henry Wimbush.

'Look at them, sir,' he said, with a motion of his hand towards the wallowing swine. 'Rightly is they called pigs.'

'Rightly indeed,' Mr Wimbush agreed.

'I am abashed by that man,' said Mr Scogan, as old Rowley plodded off slowly and with dignity. 'What wisdom, what judgment, what a sense of values! "Rightly are they called swine." Yes. And I wish I could, with as much justice, say, "Rightly are we called men."'

They walked on towards the cowsheds and the stables of the cart-horses. Five white geese, taking the air this fine morning, even as they were doing, met them in the way. They hesitated, cackled; then, converting their lifted necks into rigid, horizontal snakes, they rushed off in disorder, hissing horribly as they went. Red calves paddled in the dung and mud of a spacious yard. In another enclosure stood the bull, massive as a locomotive. He was a very calm bull, and his face wore an expression of melancholy stupidity. He gazed with reddish-brown eyes at his visitors, chewed thoughtfully at the tangible memories of an earlier meal, swallowed and regurgitated, chewed again. His tail lashed savagely from side to side; it seemed to have nothing to do with his impassive bulk. Between his short horns was a triangle of red curls, short and dense.

'Splendid animal,' said Henry Wimbush. 'Pedigree stock. But he's getting a little old, like the boar.'

'Fat him up and slaughter him,' Mr Scogan pronounced, with a delicate old-maidish precision of utterance.

'Couldn't you give the animals a little holiday from producing children?' asked Anne. 'I'm sorry for the poor things.'

Mr Wimbush shook his head. 'Personally,' he said, 'I rather like seeing fourteen pigs grow where only one grew before. The spectacle of so much crude life is refreshing.'

'I'm glad to hear you say so,' Gombauld broke in warmly. 'Lots of life : that's what we want. I like pullulation; everything ought to increase and multiply as hard as it can.'

Gombauld grew lyrical. Everybody ought to have children – Anne ought to have them, Mary ought to have them – dozens and dozens. He emphasized his point by thumping with his walking-stick on the bull's leather flanks. Mr Scogan ought to pass on his intelligence to little Scogans, and Denis to little Denises. The bull turned his head to see what was happening, regarded the drumming stick for several seconds, then turned back again satisfied, it seemed, that nothing was happening. Sterility was odious, unnatural, a sin against life. Life, life, and still more life. The ribs of the placid bull resounded.

Standing with his back against the farmyard pump, a little apart, Denis examined the group. Gombauld, passionate and vivacious, was its centre. The others stood round, listening – Henry Wimbush, calm and polite beneath his grey bowler; Mary, with parted lips and eyes that shone with the indignation of a convinced birth-controller. Anne looked on through half-shut eyes, smiling; and beside her stood Mr Scogan, bolt upright in an attitude of metallic rigidity that contrasted strangely with that fluid grace of hers which even in stillness suggested a soft movement.

Gombauld ceased talking, and Mary, flushed and outraged, opened her mouth to refute him. But she was too slow. Before she could utter a word Mr Scogan's fluty voice had

26

pronounced the opening phrases of a discourse. There was no hope of getting so much as a word in edgeways; Mary had perforce to resign herself.

'Even your eloquence, my dear Gombauld,' he was saying – 'even your eloquence must prove inadequate to reconvert the world to a belief in the delights of mere multiplication. With the gramophone, the cinema, and the automatic pistol, the goddess of Applied Science has presented the world with another gift, more precious even than these – the means of dissociating love from propagation. Eros, for those who wish it, is now an entirely free god; his deplorable associations with Lucina may be broken at will. In the course of the next few centuries, who knows? the world may see a more complete severance. I look forward to it optimistically. Where the great Erasmus Darwin and Miss Anna Seward, Swan of Lichfield, experimented – and, for all their scientific ardour, failed – our descendants will experiment and succeed. An impersonal generation will take the place of Nature's hideous system. In vast state incubators, rows upon rows of gravid bottles will supply the world with the population it requires. The family system will disappear; society, sapped at its very base, will have to find new foundations; and Eros, beautifully and irresponsibly free, will flit like a gay butterfly from flower to flower through a sunlit world.'

'It sounds lovely,' said Anne.

'The distant future always does.'

Mary's china blue eyes, more serious and more astonished than ever, were fixed on Mr Scogan. 'Bottles?' she said. 'Do you really think so? Bottles. . . ,'

CHAPTER VI

Mr Barbecue-Smith arrived in time for tea on Saturday afternoon. He was a short and corpulent man, with a very large head and no neck. In his earlier middle age he had been distressed by this absence of neck, but was comforted by reading in Balzac's *Louis Lambert* that all the world's great men have been marked by the same peculiarity, and for a simple and obvious reason : Greatness is nothing more nor less than the harmonious functioning of the faculties of the head and heart; the shorter the neck, the more closely these two organs approach one another; *argal* . . . It was convincing.

Mr Barbecue-Smith belonged to the old school of journalists. He sported a leonine head with a greyish-black mane of oddly unappetizing hair brushed back from a broad but low forehead. And somehow he always seemed slightly, ever so slightly, soiled. In younger days he had gaily called himself a Bohemian. He did so no longer. He was a teacher now, a kind of prophet. Some of his books of comfort and spiritual teaching were in their hundred and twentieth thousand.

Priscilla received him with every mark of esteem. He had never been to Crome before; she showed him round the house. Mr Barbecue-Smith was full of admiration.

'So quaint, so old-world,' he kept repeating. He had a rich, rather unctuous voice.

Priscilla praised his latest book. 'Splendid, I thought it was,' she said in her large, jolly way.

'I'm happy to think you found it a comfort,' said Mr Barbecue-Smith.

'Oh, tremendously ! And the bit about the Lotus Pool – I thought that so beautiful.'

'I knew you would like that. It came to me, you know, from without.' He waved his hand to indicate the astral world.

They went out into the garden for tea. Mr Barbecue-Smith was duly introduced.

'Mr Stone is a writer too,' said Priscilla, as she introduced Denis.

28

'Indeed!' Mr Barbecue-Smith smiled benignly, and looking up at Denis with an expression of Olympian condescension, 'And what sort of things do you write?'

Denis was furious, and, to make matters worse, he felt himself blushing hotly. Had Priscilla no sense of proportion? She was putting them in the same category – Barbecue-Smith and himself. They were both writers, they both used pen and ink. To Mr Barbecue-Smith's question he answered, 'Oh, nothing much, nothing,' and looked away.

'Mr Stone is one of our younger poets.' It was Anne's voice. He scowled at her, and she smiled back exasperatingly.

'Excellent, excellent,' said Mr Barbecue-Smith, and he squeezed Denis's arm encouragingly. 'The Bard's is a noble calling.'

As soon as tea was over Mr Barbecue-Smith excused himself; he had to do some writing before dinner. Priscilla quite understood. The prophet retired to his chamber.

Mr Barbecue-Smith came down to the drawing-room at ten to eight. He was in a good humour, and, as he descended the stairs, he smiled to himself and rubbed his large white hands together. In the drawing-room someone was playing softly and ramblingly on the piano. He wondered who it could be. One of the young ladies, perhaps. But no, it was only Denis, who got up hurriedly and, with some embarrassment as he came into the room.

'Do go on, do go on,' said Mr Barbecue-Smith. 'I am very fond of music.'

'Then I couldn't possibly go on,' Denis replied. 'I only make noises.'

There was a silence. Mr Barbecue-Smith stood with his back to the hearth, warming himself at the memory of last winter's fires. He could not control his interior satisfaction, but still went on smiling to himself. At last he turned to Denis.

'You write,' he asked, 'don't you?'

'Well, yes – a little, you know.'

'How many words do you find you can write in an hour?'

'I don't think I've ever counted.'

'Oh, you ought to, you ought to. It's most important.'

Denis exercised his memory. 'When I'm in good form,' he said, 'I fancy I do a twelve-hundred word review in about four hours. But sometimes it takes me much longer.'

Mr Barbecue-Smith nodded. 'Yes, three hundred words an hour at your best.' He walked out into the middle of the room, turned round on his heels, and confronted Denis again. 'Guess how many words I wrote this evening between five and half-past seven.'

'I can't imagine.'

'No, but you must guess. Between five and half-past seven – that's two and a half hours.'

'Twelve hundred words,' Denis hazarded.

'No, no, no.' Mr Barbecue-Smith's expanded face shone with gaiety. 'Try again.'

'Fifteen hundred.'

'No.'

'I give it up,' said Denis. He found he couldn't summon up much interest in Mr Barbecue-Smith's writing.

'Well, I'll tell you. Three thousand eight hundred.'

Denis opened his eyes. 'You must get a lot done in a day,' he said.

Mr Barbecue-Smith suddenly became extremely confidential. He pulled up a stool to the side of Denis's arm-chair, sat down in it, and began to talk softly and rapidly.

'Listen to me,' he said, laying his hand on Denis's sleeve. 'You want to make your living by writing; you're young, you're inexperienced. Let me give you a little sound advice.'

What was the fellow going to do? Denis wondered : give him an introduction to the editor of *John o' London's Weekly*, or tell him where he could sell a light middle for seven guineas? Mr Barbecue-Smith patted his arm several times and went on.

'The secret of writing,' he said, breathing it into the young man's ear – 'the secret of writing is Inspiration.'

Denis looked at him in astonishment.

'Inspiration . . .' Mr Barbecue-Smith repeated.

'You mean the native wood-note business?'

Mr Barbecue-Smith nodded.

'Oh, then I entirely agree with you,' said Denis. 'But what if one hasn't got Inspiration?'

'That was precisely the question I was waiting for,' said Mr Barbecue-Smith. 'You ask me what one should do if one hasn't got Inspiration. I answer : you have Inspiration;

everyone has Inspiration. It's simply a question of getting it to function.'

The clock struck eight. There was no sign of any of the other guests; everybody was always late at Crome. Mr Barbecue-Smith went on.

'That's my secret,' he said. 'I give it you freely.' (Denis made a suitably grateful murmur and grimace.) 'I'll help you to find your Inspiration, because I don't like to see a nice, steady young man like you exhausting his vitality and wasting the best years of his life in a grinding intellectual labour that could be completely obviated by Inspiration. I did it myself, so I know what it's like. Up till the time I was thirty-eight I was a writer like you – a writer without Inspiration. All I wrote I squeezed out of myself by sheer hard work. Why, in those days I was never able to do more than six-fifty words an hour, and what's more, I often didn't sell what I wrote.' He sighed. 'We artists,' he said parenthetically, 'we intellectuals aren't much appreciated here in England.' Denis wondered if there was any method, consistent, of course, with politeness, by which he could dissociate himself from Mr Barbecue-Smith's 'we.' There was none; and besides, it was too late now, for Mr Barbecue-Smith was once more pursuing the tenor of his discourse.

'At thirty-eight I was a poor, struggling, tired, over-worked, unknown journalist. Now, at fifty . . .' He paused modestly and made a little gesture, moving his fat hands outwards, away from one another, and expanding his fingers as though in demonstration. He was exhibiting himself. Denis thought of that advertisement of Nestlé's milk – the two cats on the wall, under the moon, one black and thin, the other white, sleek, and fat. Before Inspiration and after.

'Inspiration has made the difference,' said Mr Barbecue-Smith solemnly. 'It came quite suddenly – like a gentle dew from heaven.' He lifted his hand and let it fall back on to his knee to indicate the descent of the dew. 'It was one evening. I was writing my first book about the Conduct of Life – *Humble Heroisms*. You may have read it; it has been a comfort – at least I hope and think so – a comfort to many thousands. I was in the middle of the second chapter, and I was stuck. Fatigue, overwork – I had only written a hundred words in the last hour, and I could get no further. I sat biting the end of my pen and looking at the electric light, which hung above my table, a little above and in front of me.' He indicated the position of the lamp with elaborate care. 'Have you ever looked at a bright light intently for a long time?' he asked, turning to Denis. Denis didn't think he had. 'You can hypnotize yourself that way,' Mr Barbecue-Smith went on.

The gong sounded in a terrific crescendo from the hall. Still no sign of the others. Denis was horribly hungry.

'That's what happened to me,' said Mr Barbecue-Smith. 'I was hypnotized. I lost consciousness like that.' He snapped his fingers. 'When I came to, I found that it was past midnight, and I had written four thousand words. Four thousand,' he repeated, opening his mouth very wide on the *ou* of thousand. 'Inspiration had come to me.'

'What a very extraordinary thing,' said Denis.

'I was afraid of it at first. It didn't seem to me natural. I didn't feel, somehow, that it was quite right, quite fair, I might almost say, to produce a literary composition unconsciously. Besides, I was afraid I might have written nonsense.'

'And had you written nonsense?' Denis asked.

'Certainly not,' Mr Barbecue-Smith replied, with a trace of annoyance. 'Certainly not. It was admirable. Just a few spelling mistakes and slips, such as there generally are in automatic writing. But the style, the thought – all the essentials were admirable. After that, Inspiration came to me regularly. I wrote the whole of *Humble Heroisms* like that. It was a great success, and so has everything been that I have written since.' He leaned forward and jabbed at Denis with his finger. 'That's my secret,' he said, 'and that's how you could write too, if you tried – without effort, fluently, well.'

'But how?' asked Denis, trying not to show how deeply he had been insulted by that final 'well.'

'By cultivating your Inspiration, by getting into touch with your Subconscious. Have you ever read my little book, *Pipe-Lines to the Infinite*?'

Denis had to confess that that was, precisely, one of the few, perhaps the only one, of Mr Barbecue-Smith's works he had not read.

'Never mind, never mind,' said Mr Barbecue-Smith. 'It's just a little book about the connection of the Subconscious with the Infinite. Get into touch with the Subconscious and you are in touch with the Universe. Inspiration, in fact. You follow me?'

'Perfectly, perfectly,' said Denis. 'But don't you find that the Universe sometimes sends you very irrelevant messages?'

'I don't allow it to,' Mr Barbecue-Smith replied. 'I canalize it. I bring it down through pipes to work the turbines of my conscious mind.'

'Like Niagara,' Denis suggested. Some of Mr Barbecue-Smith's remarks sounded strangely like quotations – quotations from his own works, no doubt.

'Precisely. Like Niagara. And this is how I do it.' He leaned forward, and with a raised forefinger marked his points as he made them, beating time, as it were, to his discourse. 'Before I go off into my trance, I concentrate on the subject I wish to be inspired about. Let us say I am writing about the humble heroisms; for ten minutes before I go into the trance I think of nothing but orphans supporting their little brothers and sisters, of dull work well and patiently done, and I focus my mind on such great philosophical truths as the purification and uplifting of the soul by suffering, and the alchemical transformation of leaden evil into golden good.' (Denis again hung up his little festoon of quotation marks.) 'Then I pop off. Two or three hours later I wake up again, and find that inspiration has done its work. Thousands of words, comforting, uplifting words, lie before me. I type them out neatly on my machine and they are ready for the printer.'

'It all sounds wonderfully simple,' said Denis.

'It is. All the great and splendid and divine things of life are wonderfully simple.' (Quotation marks again.) 'When I have to do my aphorisms,' Mr Barbecue-Smith continued, 'I prelude my trance by turning over the pages of any Dictionary of Quotations or Shakespeare Calendar that comes to hand. That sets the key, so to speak; that ensures that the Universe shall come flowing in, not in a continuous rush, but in aphorismic drops. You see the idea?'

Denis nodded. Mr Barbecue-Smith put his hand in his pocket and pulled out a notebook. 'I did a few in the train today,' he said, turning over the pages. 'Just dropped off into a trance in a corner of my carriage. I find the train very conducive to good work. Here they are.' He cleared his throat and read :

'*The Mountain Road may be steep, but the air is pure up there, and it is from the Summit that one gets the view.*'

'*The Things that Really Matter happen in the Heart.*'

It was curious, Denis reflected, the way the Infinite sometimes repeated itself.

'*Seeing is Believing. Yes, but Believing is also Seeing. If I believe in God, I see God, even in the things that seem to be evil.*'

Mr Barbecue-Smith looked up from his notebook. 'That last one,' he said, 'is particularly subtle and beautiful, don't you think? Without Inspiration I could never have hit on that.' He re-read the apophthegm with a slower and more solemn utterance. 'Straight from the Infinite,' he commented reflectively, then addressed himself to the next aphorism.

'*The flame of a candle gives Light, but it also Burns.*'

Puzzled wrinkles appeared on Mr Barbecue-Smith's forehead. 'I don't exactly know what that means,' he said. 'It's very gnomic. One could apply it, of course, to the Higher Education – illuminating, but provoking the Lower Classes to discontent and revolution. Yes, I suppose that's what it is. But it's gnomic, it's gnomic.' He rubbed his chin thoughtfully. The gong sounded again, clamorously, it seemed imploringly : dinner was growing cold. It roused Mr Barbecue-Smith from meditation. He turned to Denis.

'You understand me now when I advise you to cultivate your Inspiration. Let your Subconscious work for you; turn on the Niagara of the Infinite.'

There was the sound of feet on the stairs. Mr Barbecue-Smith got up, laid his hand for an instant on Denis's shoulder, and said :

'No more now. Another time. And remember, I rely absolutely on your discretion in this matter. There are intimate, sacred things that one doesn't wish to be generally known.'

'Of course,' said Denis. 'I quite understand.'

CHAPTER VII

At Crome all the beds were ancient hereditary pieces of furniture. Huge beds, like four-masted ships, with furled sails
of shining coloured stuff. Beds carved and inlaid, beds
painted and gilded. Beds of walnut and oak, of rare exotic
woods. Beds of every date and fashion from the time of Sir
Ferdinando, who built the house, to the time of his namesake
in the late eighteenth century, the last of the family, but all
of them grandiose, magnificent.

The finest of all was now Anne's bed. Sir Julius, son to Sir
Ferdinand, had had it made in Venice against his wife's
first lying-in. Early *seicento* Venice had expended all its extravagant art in the making of it. The body of the bed was
like a great square sarcophagus. Clustering roses were carved
in high relief on its wooden panels, and luscious *putti* wallowed among the roses. On the black groundwork of the
panels the carved reliefs were gilded and burnished. The
golden roses twined in spirals up the four pillar-like posts,
and cherubs, seated at the top of each column, supported a
wooden canopy fretted with the same carved flowers.

Anne was reading in bed. Two candles stood on the little
table beside her. In their rich light her face, her bare arm
and shoulder took on warm hues and a sort of peach-like
quality of surface. Here and there in the canopy above her
carved golden petals shone brightly among profound
shadows, and the soft light, falling on the sculptured panel of
the bed, broke restlessly among the intricate roses, lingered in
a broad caress on the blown cheeks, the dimpled bellies, the
tight, absurd little posteriors of the sprawling *putti*.

There was a discreet tap at the door. She looked up.
'Come in, come in.' A face, round and childish within its
sleek bell of golden hair, peered round the opening door.
More childish-looking still, a suit of mauve pyjamas made
its entrance.

It was Mary. 'I thought I'd just look in for a moment to
say good-night,' she said, and sat down on the edge of the
bed.

35

Anne closed her book. 'That was very sweet of you.'

'What are you reading?' She looked at the book. 'Rather second-rate, isn't it?' The tone in which Mary pronounced the word 'second-rate' implied an almost infinite denigration. She was accustomed in London to associate only with first-rate people who liked first-rate things, and she knew that there were very, very few first-rate things in the world, and that those were mostly French.

'Well, I'm afraid I like it,' said Anne. There was nothing more to be said. The silence that followed was a rather uncomfortable one. Mary fiddled uneasily with the bottom button of her pyjama jacket. Leaning back on her mound of heaped-up pillows, Anne waited and wondered what was coming.

'I'm so awfully afraid of repressions,' said Mary at last, bursting suddenly and surprisingly into speech. She pronounced the words on the tail-end of an expiring breath, and had to gasp for new air almost before the phrase was finished.

'What's there to be depressed about?'

'I said repressions, not depressions.'

'Oh, repressions; I see,' said Anne. 'But repressions of what?'

Mary had to explain. 'The natural instincts of sex . . .' she began didactically. But Anne cut her short.

'Yes, yes. Perfectly. I understand. Repressions; old maids and all the rest. But what about them?'

'That's just it,' said Mary. 'I'm afraid of them. It's always dangerous to repress one's instincts. I'm beginning to detect in myself symptoms like the ones you read of in the books. I constantly dream that I'm falling down wells; and sometimes I even dream that I'm climbing up ladders. It's most disquieting. The symptoms are only too clear.'

'Are they?'

'One may become a nymphomaniac if one's not careful. You've no idea how serious these repressions are if you don't get rid of them in time.'

'It sounds too awful,' said Anne. 'But I don't see that I can do anything to help you.'

'I thought I'd just like to talk it over with you.'

'Why, of course; I'm only too happy, Mary darling.'

Mary coughed and drew a deep breath. 'I presume,' she

began sententiously, 'I presume we may take for granted that an intelligent young woman of twenty-three who has lived in civilized society in the twentieth century has no prejudices.'

'Well, I confess I still have a few.'

'But not about repressions.'

'No, not many about repressions; that's true.'

'Or, rather, about getting rid of repressions.'

'Exactly.'

'So much for our fundamental postulate,' said Mary. Solemnity was expressed in every feature of her round young face, radiated from her large blue eyes. 'We come next to the desirability of possessing experience. I hope we are agreed that knowledge is desirable and that ignorance is undesirable.'

Obedient as one of those complaisant disciples from whom Socrates could get whatever answer he chose, Anne gave her assent to this proposition.

'And we are equally agreed, I hope, that marriage is what it is.'

'It is.'

'Good!' said Mary. 'And repressions being what they are ...'

'Exactly.'

'There would therefore seem to be only one conclusion.'

'But I knew that,' Anne exclaimed, 'before you began.'

'Yes, but now it's been proved,' said Mary. 'One must do things logically. The question is now ...'

'But where does the question come in? You've reached your only possible conclusion – logically, which is more than I could have done. All that remains is to impart the information to someone you like – someone you like really rather a lot, someone you're in love with, if I may express myself so baldly.'

'But that's just where the question comes in,' Mary exclaimed. 'I'm not in love with anybody.'

'Then, if I were you, I should wait till you are.'

'But I can't go on dreaming night after night that I'm falling down a well. It's too dangerous.'

'Well, if it really is *too* dangerous, then of course you must do something about it; you must find somebody else.'

'But who?' A thoughtful frown puckered Mary's brow. 'It

must be somebody intelligent, somebody with intellectual interests that I can share. And it must be somebody with a proper respect for women, somebody who's prepared to talk seriously about his work and his ideas and about my work and my ideas. It isn't, as you see, at all easy to find the right person.'

'Well,' said Anne, 'there are three unattached and intelligent men in the house at the present time. There's Mr Scogan, to begin with; but perhaps he's rather too much of a genuine antique. And there are Gombauld and Denis. Shall we say that the choice is limited to the last two?'

Mary nodded. 'I think we had better,' she said, and then hesitated, with a certain air of embarrassment.

'What is it?'

'I was wondering,' said Mary, with a gasp, 'whether they really were unattached. I thought that perhaps you might . . . you might . . .'

'It was very nice of you to think of me, Mary darling,' said Anne, smiling the tight cat's smile. 'But as far as I'm concerned, they are both entirely unattached.'

'I'm very glad of that,' said Mary, looking relieved. 'We are now confronted with the question : Which of the two?'

'I can give no advice. It's a matter for your taste.'

'It's not a matter of my taste,' Mary pronounced, 'but of their merits. We must weigh them and consider them carefully and dispassionately.'

'You must do the weighing yourself,' said Anne; there was still the trace of a smile at the corners of her mouth and round the half-closed eyes. 'I won't run the risk of advising you wrongly.'

'Gombauld has more talent,' Mary began, 'but he is less civilized than Denis.' Mary's pronunciation of 'civilized' gave the word a special and additional significance. She uttered it meticulously, in the very front of her mouth, hissing delicately on the opening sibilant. So few people were civilized, and they, like the first-rate works of art, were mostly French. 'Civilization is most important, don't you think?'

Anne held up her hand. 'I won't advise,' she said. 'You must make the decision.'

'Gombauld's family,' Mary went on reflectively, 'comes from Marseilles. Rather a dangerous heredity, when one

38

thinks of the Latin attitude towards women. But then, I sometimes wonder whether Denis is altogether serious-minded, whether he isn't rather a dilettante. It's very difficult. What do you think?'

'I'm not listening,' said Anne. 'I refuse to take any responsibility.'

Mary sighed. 'Well,' she said, 'I think I had better go to bed and think about it.'

'Carefully and dispassionately,' said Anne.

At the door Mary turned round. 'Good-night,' she said, and wondered as she said the words why Anne was smiling in that curious way. It was probably nothing, she reflected. Anne often smiled for no apparent reason; it was probably just a habit. 'I hope I shan't dream of falling down wells again tonight,' she added.

'Ladders are worse,' said Anne.

Mary nodded. 'Yes, ladders are much graver.'

CHAPTER VIII

Breakfast on Sunday morning was an hour later than on week-days, and Priscilla, who usually made no public appearance before luncheon, honoured it by her presence. Dressed in black silk, with a ruby cross as well as her customary string of pearls round her neck, she presided. An enormous Sunday paper concealed all but the extreme pinnacle of her coiffure from the outer world.

'I see Surrey has won,' she said, with her mouth full, 'by four wickets. The sun is in Leo : that would account for it !'

'Splendid game, cricket,' remarked Mr Barbecue-Smith heartily to no one in particular; 'so thoroughly English.'

Jenny, who was sitting next to him, woke up suddenly with a start. 'What?' she said. 'What?'

'So English,' repeated Mr Barbecue-Smith.

Jenny looked at him, surprised. 'English? Of course I am.'

He was beginning to explain, when Mrs Wimbush vailed her Sunday paper, and appeared, a square, mauve-powdered face in the midst of orange splendours. 'I see there's a new series of articles on the next world just beginning,' she said to Mr Barbecue-Smith. 'This one's called "Summer Land and Gehenna."'

'Summer Land,' echoed Mr Barbecue-Smith, closing his eyes. 'Summer Land. A beautiful name. Beautiful – beautiful.'

Mary had taken the seat next to Denis's. After a night of careful consideration she had decided on Denis. He might have less talent than Gombauld, he might be a little lacking in seriousness, but somehow he was safer.

'Are you writing much poetry here in the country?' she asked, with a bright gravity.

'None,' said Denis curtly. 'I haven't brought my typewriter.'

'But do you mean to say you can't write without a typewriter?'

Denis shook his head. He hated talking at breakfast, and,

besides, he wanted to hear what Mr Scogan was saying at the other end of the table.

'. . . My scheme for dealing with the Church,' Mr Scogan was saying, 'is beautifully simple. At the present time the Anglican clergy wear their collars the wrong way round. I would compel them to wear, not only their collars, but all their clothes, turned back to front – coat, waistcoat, trousers, boots – so that every clergyman should present to the world a smooth façade, unbroken by stud, button, or lace. The enforcement of such a livery would act as a wholesome deterrent to those intending to enter the Church. At the same time it would enormously enhance, what Archbishop Laud so rightly insisted on, the "beauty of holiness" in the few incorrigibles who could not be deterred.'

'In hell, it seems,' said Priscilla, reading in her Sunday paper, 'the children amuse themselves by flaying lambs alive.'

'Ah, but, dear lady, that's only a symbol,' exclaimed Mr Barbecue-Smith, 'a material symbol of a h-piritual truth. Lambs signify . . .'

'Then there are military uniforms,' Mr Scogan went on. 'When scarlet and pipeclay were abandoned for khaki, there were some who trembled for the future of war. But then, finding how elegant the new tunic was, how closely it clipped the waist, how voluptuously, with the lateral bustles of the pockets, it exaggerated the hips; when they realized the brilliant potentialities of breeches and top-boots, they were reassured. Abolish these military elegances, standardize a uniform of sack-cloth and mackintosh, you will very soon find that . . .'

'Is anyone coming to church with me this morning?' asked Henry Wimbush. No one responded. He baited his bare invitation. 'I read the lessons, you know. And there's Mr Bodiham. His sermons are sometimes worth hearing.'

'Thank you, thank you,' said Mr Barbecue-Smith. 'I for one prefer to worship in the infinite church of Nature. How does our Shakespeare put it? "Sermons in books, stones in the running brooks."' He waved his arm in a fine gesture towards the window, and even as he did so he became vaguely, but none the less insistently, none the less uncomfortably aware that something had gone wrong with the quotation. Something – what could it be? Sermons? Stones? Books?

CHAPTER IX

Mr Bodiham was sitting in his study at the Rectory. The nineteenth-century Gothic windows, narrow and pointed, admitted the light grudgingly; in spite of the brilliant July weather, the room was sombre. Brown varnished bookshelves lined the walls, filled with row upon row of those thick, heavy theological works which the second-hand booksellers generally sell by weight. The mantelpiece, the overmantel, a towering structure of spindly pillars and little shelves, were brown and varnished. The writing-desk was brown and varnished. So were the chairs, so was the door. A dark red-brown carpet with patterns covered the floor. Everything was brown in the room, and there was a curious brownish smell.

In the midst of this brown gloom Mr Bodiham sat at his desk. He was the man in the Iron Mask. A grey metallic face with iron cheek-bones and a narrow iron brow; iron folds, hard and unchanging, ran perpendicularly down his cheeks; his nose was the iron beak of some thin, delicate bird of rapine. He had brown eyes, set in sockets rimmed with iron; round them the skin was dark, as though it had been charred. Dense wiry hair covered his skull; it had been black, it was turning grey. His ears were very small and fine. His jaws, his chin, his upper lip were dark, iron-dark, where he had shaved. His voice, when he spoke and especially when he raised it in preaching, was harsh, like the grating of iron hinges when a seldom-used door is opened.

It was nearly half-past twelve. He had just come back from church, hoarse and weary with preaching. He preached with fury, with passion, an iron man beating with a flail upon the souls of his congregation. But the souls of the faithful at Crome were made of india-rubber, solid rubber; the flail rebounded. They were used to Mr Bodiham at Crome. The flail thumped on india-rubber, and as often as not the rubber slept.

That morning he had preached, as he had often preached before, on the nature of God. He had tried to make them understand about God, what a fearful thing it is to fall into

42

His hands. God – they thought of something soft and merciful. They blinded themselves to facts; still more, they blinded themselves to the Bible. The passengers on the *Titanic* sang 'Nearer my God to Thee' as the ship was going down. Did they realize what they were asking to be brought nearer to? A white fire of righteousness, an angry fire. . . .

When Savonarola preached, men sobbed and groaned aloud. Nothing broke the polite silence with which Crome listened to Mr Bodiham – only an occasional cough and sometimes the sound of heavy breathing. In the front pew sat Henry Wimbush, calm, well-bred, beautifully dressed. There were times when Mr Bodiham wanted to jump down from the pulpit and shake him into life, – times when he would have liked to beat and kill his whole congregation.

He sat at his desk dejectedly. Outside the Gothic windows the earth was warm and marvellously calm. Everything was as it had always been. And yet, and yet . . . It was nearly four years now since he had preached that sermon on Matthew xxiv. 7 : 'For nation shall rise up against nation, and kingdom against kingdom : and there shall be famines, and pestilences, and earthquakes, in divers places.' It was nearly four years. He had had the sermon printed; it was so terribly, so vitally important that all the world should know what he had to say. A copy of the little pamphlet lay on his desk – eight small grey pages, printed by a fount of type that had grown blunt, like an old dog's teeth, by the endless champing and champing of the press. He opened it and began to read it yet once again.

' "For nation shall rise up against nation, and kingdom against kingdom : and there shall be famines, and pestilences, and earthquakes, in divers places." '

'Nineteen centuries have elapsed since Our Lord gave utterance to those words, and not a single one of them has been without wars, plagues, famines, and earthquakes. Mighty empires have crashed in ruin to the ground, diseases have unpeopled half the globe, there have been vast natural cataclysms in which thousands have been overwhelmed by flood and fire and whirlwind. Time and again, in the course of these nineteen centuries, such things have happened, but they have not brought Christ back to earth. They were "signs of the times" inasmuch as they were signs of God's wrath

43

against the chronic wickedness of mankind, but they were not signs of the times in connection with the Second Coming.

'If earnest Christians have regarded the present war as a true sign of the Lord's approaching return, it is not merely because it happens to be a great war involving the lives of millions of people, not merely because famine is tightening its grip on every country in Europe, not merely because disease of every kind, from syphilis to spotted fever, is rife among the warring nations; no, it is not for these reasons that we regard this war as a true Sign of the Times, but because in its origin and its progress it is marked by certain characteristics which seem to connect it almost beyond a doubt with the predictions in Christian Prophecy relating to the Second Coming of the Lord.

'Let me enumerate the features of the present war which most clearly suggest that it is a Sign foretelling the near approach of the Second Advent. Our Lord said that "this Gospel of the Kingdom shall be preached in all the world for a witness unto all nations; and then shall the end come." Although it would be presumptuous for us to say what degree of evangelization will be regarded by God as sufficient, we may at least confidently hope that a century of unflagging missionary work has brought the fulfilment of this condition at any rate near. True, the larger number of the world's inhabitants have remained deaf to the preaching of the true religion; but that does not vitiate the fact that the Gospel *has* been preached "for a witness" to all unbelievers from the Papist to the Zulu. The responsibility for the continued prevalence of unbelief lies, not with the preachers, but with those preached to.

'Again, it has been generally recognized that "the drying up of the waters of the great river Euphrates," mentioned in the sixteenth chapter of Revelations, refers to the decay and extinction of Turkish power, and is a sign of the near approaching end of the world as we know it. The capture of Jerusalem and the successes in Mesopotamia are great strides forward in the destruction of the Ottoman Empire; though it must be admitted that the Gallipoli episode proved that the Turk still possesses a "notable horn" of strength. Historically speaking, this drying up of Ottoman power has been going on for the past century; the last two years have witnessed a great acceleration of the process, and there can be no doubt that complete desiccation is within sight.

'Closely following on the words concerning the drying up of Euphrates comes the prophecy of Armageddon, that world war with which the Second Coming is to be so closely associated. Once begun, the world war can end only with the return of Christ, and His coming will be sudden and unexpected, like that of a thief in the night.

'Let us examine the facts. In history, exactly as in St John's Gospel, the world war is immediately preceded by the drying up of Euphrates, or the decay of Turkish power. This fact alone would be enough to connect the present conflict with the Armageddon of Revelations and therefore to point to the near approach of the Second Advent. But further evidence of an even more solid and convincing nature can be adduced.

'Armageddon is brought about by the activities of three unclean spirits, as it were toads, which come out of the mouths of the Dragon, the Beast, and the False Prophet. If we can identify these three powers of evil much light will clearly be thrown on the whole question.

'The Dragon, the Beast, and the False Prophet can all be identified in history. Satan, who can only work through human agency, has used these three powers in the long war against Christ which has filled the last nineteen centuries with religious strife. The Dragon, it has been sufficiently established, is pagan Rome, and the spirit issuing from its mouth is the spirit of Infidelity. The Beast, alternatively symbolized as a Woman, is undoubtedly the Papal power, and Popery is the spirit which it spews forth. There is only one power which answers to the description of the False Prophet, the wolf in sheep's clothing, the agent of the devil working in the guise of the Lamb, and that power is the so-called "Society of Jesus." The spirit that issues from the mouth of the False Prophet is the spirit of False Morality.

'We may assume, then, that the three evil spirits are Infidelity, Popery, and False Morality. Have these three influences been the real cause of the present conflict? The answer is clear.

'The spirit of Infidelity is the very spirit of German criticism. The Higher Criticism, as it is mockingly called, denies the possibility of miracles, prediction, and real inspiration, and attempts to account for the Bible as a natural development. Slowly but surely, during the last eighty years, the spirit of Infidelity has been robbing the Germans of their Bible and their faith, so that Germany is today a nation of unbelievers. Higher Criticism has thus made the war possible; for it would be absolutely impossible for any Christian nation to wage war as Germany is waging it.

'We come next to the spirit of Popery, whose influence in causing the war was quite as great as that of Infidelity, though not, perhaps, so immediately obvious. Since the Franco-Prussian War the Papal power has steadily declined in France, while in Germany it has steadily increased. Today France is an anti-papal state, while Germany possesses a powerful Roman Catholic minority. Two papally controlled states, Germany and Austria, are at war with six anti-papal states – England, France, Italy, Russia, Serbia, and Portugal. Belgium is, of course, a thoroughly papal state, and there can be little doubt that the presence on the Allies' side of an element so essentially hostile has done much to hamper the righteous cause and is responsible for our comparative ill-success. That the spirit of Popery is behind the war is thus seen clearly enough in the grouping of the opposed powers, while the rebellion in the Roman Catholic parts of Ireland has merely confirmed a conclusion already obvious to any unbiased mind.

'The spirit of False Morality has played as great a part in this war as the two other evil spirits. The Scrap of Paper incident is the nearest and most obvious example of Germany's adherence to this essentially unchristian or Jesuitical morality. The end is German world-power, and in the attainment of this end, any means are justifiable. It is the true principle of Jesuitry applied to international politics.

'The identification is now complete. As was predicted in Revelations, the three evil spirits have gone forth just as the decay of the Ottoman power was nearing completion, and have joined together to make the world war. The warning, "Behold, I come as a thief," is therefore meant for the present period – for you and me and all the world. This war will lead on inevitably to the war of Armageddon, and will only be brought to an end by the Lord's personal return.

'And when He returns, what will happen? Those who are in Christ, St John tells us, will be called to the Supper of the Lamb. Those who are found fighting against Him will be called to the Supper of the Great God – that grim banquet where they shall not feast, but be feasted on. "For," as St John says, "I saw an angel standing in the sun; and he cried in a loud voice, saying to all the fowls that fly in the midst of heaven, Come and gather yourselves together unto the supper of the Great God; that ye may eat the flesh of kings, and the flesh of captains, and the flesh of mighty men, and the flesh of horses, and of them that sit on them, and the flesh of all men, both free and bond, both small and great." All the enemies of Christ will be slain with the sword of him that sits upon the horse, "and all the fowls will be filled with their flesh." That is the Supper of the Great God.

'It may be soon or it may, as men reckon time, be long; but sooner or later, inevitably, the Lord will come and deliver the world from its present troubles. And woe unto them who are called, not to the Supper of the Lamb, but to the Supper of the Great God. They will realize then, but too late, that God is a God of Wrath as well as a God of Forgiveness. The God who sent bears to devour the mockers of Elisha, the God who smote the Egyptians for their stubborn wickedness, will assuredly smite them too, unless they make haste to repent. But perhaps it is already too late. Who knows but that tomorrow, in a moment even, Christ may be upon us unawares, like a thief? In a little while, who knows? the angel standing in the sun may be summoning the ravens and vultures from their crannies in the rocks to feed upon the putrefying flesh of the millions of unrighteous whom God's wrath has destroyed. Be ready, then; the coming of the Lord is at hand. May it be for all of you an object of hope, not a moment to be looked forward to with terror and trembling.'

Mr Bodiham closed the little pamphlet and leaned back in his chair. The argument was sound, absolutely compelling; and yet – it was four years since he had preached that sermon; four years, and England was at peace, the sun shone, the people of Crome were as wicked and indifferent as ever – more so, indeed, if that were possible. If only he could understand, if the heavens would but make a sign! But his questionings remained unanswered. Seated there in his

47

brown varnished chair under the Ruskinian window, he could have screamed aloud. He gripped the arms of his chair – gripping, gripping for control. The knuckles of his hands whitened; he bit his lip. In a few seconds he was able to relax the tension; he began to rebuke himself for his rebellious impatience.

Four years, he reflected; what were four years, after all? It must inevitably take a long time for Armageddon to ripen, to yeast itself up. The episode of 1914 had been a preliminary skirmish. And as for the war having come to an end – why, that, of course, was illusory. It was still going on, smouldering away in Silesia, in Ireland, in Anatolia; the discontent in Egypt and India was preparing the way, perhaps, for a great extension of the slaughter among the heathen peoples. The Chinese boycott of Japan, and the rivalries of that country and America in the Pacific, might be breeding a great new war in the East. The prospect, Mr Bodiham tried to assure himself, was hopeful; the real, the genuine Armageddon might soon begin, and then, like a thief in the night . . . But, in spite of all his comfortable reasoning, he remained unhappy, dissatisfied. Four years ago he had been so confident; God's intention seemed then so plain. And now? Now, he did well to be angry. And now he suffered too.

Sudden and silent as a phantom Mrs Bodiham appeared, gliding noiselessly across the room. Above her black dress her face was pale with an opaque whiteness, her eyes were pale as water in a glass, and her strawy hair was almost colourless. She held a large envelope in her hand.

'This came for you by the post,' she said softly.

The envelope was unsealed. Mechanically Mr Bodiham tore it open. It contained a pamphlet, larger than his own and more elegant in appearance. 'The House of Sheeny, Clerical Outfitters, Birmingham.' He turned over the pages. The catalogue was tastefully and ecclesiastically printed in antique characters with illuminated Gothic initials. Red marginal lines, crossed at the corners after the manner of an Oxford picture frame, enclosed each page of type; little red crosses took the place of full stops. Mr Bodiham turned the pages.

Soutane in best black merino. Ready to wear; in all sizes.
Clerical frock-coats. From nine guineas. A dressy garment,

tailored by our own experienced ecclesiastical cutters.

Half-tone illustrations represented young curates, some dapper, some Rugbeian and muscular, some with ascetic faces and large ecstatic eyes, dressed in jackets, in frock-coats, in surplices, in clerical evening dress, in black Norfolk suitings.

A large assortment of chasubles.

Rope girdles.

Sheeny's Special Skirt Cassocks. Tied by a string about the waist. . . . When worn under a surplice presents an appearance indistinguishable from that of a complete cassock. . . . Recommended for summer wear and hot climates.

With a gesture of horror and disgust Mr Bodiham threw the catalogue into the waste-paper basket. Mrs Bodiham looked at him; her pale, glaucous eyes reflected his action without comment.

'The village,' she said in her quiet voice, 'the village grows worse and worse every day.'

'What has happened now?' asked Mr Bodiham, feeling suddenly very weary.

'I'll tell you.' She pulled up a brown varnished chair and sat down. In the village of Crome, it seemed, Sodom and Gomorrah had come to a second birth.

The sermon attributed to '*Mr Bodiham*' in Chapter IX is a reproduction of the substance of an Address, given by the Rev. E. H. Horne, in A.D. 1916, to a meeting of clergy, and then published. It is now reprinted as an Appendix in a small book by him, entitled *The Significance of Air War* (Marshall, Morgan & Scott).

CHAPTER X

Denis did not dance, but when ragtime came squirting out
of the pianola in gushes of treacle and hot perfume, in jets of
Bengal light, then things began to dance inside him. Little
black nigger corpuscles jigged and drummed in his arteries.
He became a cage of movement, a walking *palais de danse*.
It was very uncomfortable, like the preliminary symptoms of
a disease. He sat in one of the window-seats, glumly pretending to read.

At the pianola, Henry Wimbush, smoking a long cigar
through a tunnelled pillar of amber, trod out the shattering
dance music with serene patience. Locked together, Gombauld and Anne moved with a harmoniousness that made
them seem a single creature, two-headed and four-legged. Mr
Scogan, solemnly buffoonish, shuffled round the room with
Mary. Jenny sat in the shadow behind the piano, scribbling,
so it seemed, in a big red notebook. In arm-chairs by the fireplace, Priscilla and Mr Barbecue-Smith discussed higher
things, without, apparently, being disturbed by the noise of
the Lower Plane.

'Optimism,' said Mr Barbecue-Smith, with a tone of final-
ity, speaking through strains of the 'Wild, Wild Women' –
'optimism is the opening out of the soul towards the light; it
is an expansion towards and into God, it is a h-piritual self-
unification with the Infinite.'

'How true!' sighed Priscilla, nodding the baleful splendours of her coiffure.

'Pessimism, on the other hand, is the contraction of the
soul towards darkness; it is a focusing of the self upon a point
in the Lower Plane; it is a h-piritual slavery to mere facts, to
gross physical phenomena.'

'They're making a wild man of me.' The refrain sang itself
over in Denis's mind. Yes, they were; damn them! A wild
man, but not wild enough; that was the trouble. Wild inside;
raging, writhing – yes, 'writhing' was the word, writhing
with desire. But outwardly he was hopelessly tame; outwardly – baa, baa, baa.

There they were, Anne and Gombauld, moving together as though they were a single supple creature. The beast with two backs. And he sat in a corner, pretending to read, pretending he didn't want to dance, pretending he rather despised dancing. Why? It was the baa-baa business again.

Why was he born with a different face? Why *was* he? Gombauld had a face of brass – one of those old, brazen rams that thumped against the walls of cities till they fell. He was born with a different face – a woolly face.

The music stopped. The single harmonious creature broke in two. Flushed, a little breathless, Anne swayed across the room to the pianola, laid her hand on Mr Wimbush's shoulder.

'A waltz this time, please, Uncle Henry,' she said.

'A waltz,' he repeated, and turned to the cabinet where the rolls were kept. He trod off the old roll and trod on the new, a slave at the mill, uncomplaining and beautifully well bred. 'Rum; Tum; Rum-ti-ti; Tum-ti-ti. . . .' The melody wallowed oozily along, like a ship moving forward over a sleek and oily swell. The four-legged creature, more graceful, more harmonious in its movements than ever, slid across the floor. Oh, why was he born with a different face?

'What are you reading?'

He looked up, startled. It was Mary. She had broken from the uncomfortable embrace of Mr Scogan, who had now seized on Jenny for his victim.

'What are you reading?'

'I don't know,' said Denis truthfully. He looked at the title page; the book was called *The Stock Breeder's Vade Mecum.*

'I think you are so sensible to sit and read quietly,' said Mary, fixing him with her china eyes. 'I don't know why one dances. It's so boring.'

Denis made no reply; she exacerbated him. From the armchair by the fireplace he heard Priscilla's deep voice.

'Tell me, Mr Barbecue-Smith – you know all about science, I know—' A deprecating noise came from Mr Barbecue-Smith's chair. 'This Einstein theory. It seems to upset the whole starry universe. It makes me so worried about my horoscopes. You see . . .'

Mary renewed her attack. 'Which of the contemporary poets do you like best?' she asked. Denis was filled with fury.

Why couldn't this pest of a girl leave him alone? He wanted to listen to the horrible music, to watch them dancing – oh, with what grace, as though they had been made for one another! – to savour his misery in peace. And she came and put him through this absurd catechism! She was like 'Mangold's Questions' : 'What are the three diseases of wheat?' – 'Which of the contemporary poets do you like best?'

'Blight, Mildew, and Smut,' he replied, with the laconism of one who is absolutely certain of his own mind.

It was several hours before Denis managed to go to sleep that night. Vague but agonizing miseries possessed his mind. It was not only Anne who made him miserable; he was wretched about himself, the future, life in general, the universe. 'This adolescence business,' he repeated to himself every now and then, 'is horribly boring.' But the fact that he knew his disease did not help him to cure it.

After kicking all the clothes off the bed, he got up and sought relief in composition. He wanted to imprison his nameless misery in words. At the end of an hour, nine more or less complete lines emerged from among the blots and scratchings.

'I do not know what I desire
When summer nights are dark and still,
When the wind's many-voicèd quire
Sleeps among the muffled branches.
I long and know not what I will :
And not a sound of life or laughter stanches
Time's black and silent flow.
I do not know what I desire,
I do not know.'

He read it through aloud; then threw the scribbled sheet into the waste-paper basket and got into bed again. In a very few minutes he was asleep.

CHAPTER XI

Mr Barbecue-Smith was gone. The motor had whirled him away to the station; a faint smell of burning oil commemorated his recent departure. A considerable detachment had come into the courtyard to speed him on his way; and now they were walking back, round the side of the house, towards the terrace and the garden. They walked in silence; nobody had yet ventured to comment on the departed guest.

'Well?' said Anne, at last, turning with raised inquiring eyebrows to Denis. 'Well?' It was time for someone to begin.

Denis declined the invitation; he passed it on to Mr Scogan. 'Well?' he said.

Mr Scogan did not respond; he only repeated the question, 'Well?'

It was left for Henry Wimbush to make a pronouncement. 'A very agreeable adjunct to the week-end,' he said. His tone was obituary.

They had descended, without paying much attention where they were going, the steep yew-walk that went down, under the flank of the terrace, to the pool. The house towered above them, immensely tall, with the whole height of the built-up terrace added to its own seventy feet of brick façade. The perpendicular lines of the three towers soared up, uninterrupted, enhancing the impression of height until it became overwhelming. They paused at the edge of the pool to look back.

'The man who built this house knew his business,' said Denis. 'He was an architect.'

'Was he?' said Henry Wimbush reflectively. 'I doubt it. The builder of this house was Sir Ferdinando Lapith, who flourished during the reign of Elizabeth. He inherited the estate from his father, to whom it had been granted at the time of the dissolution of the monasteries; for Crome was originally a cloister of monks and this swimming-pool their fish-pond. Sir Ferdinando was not content merely to adapt the old monastic buildings to his own purposes; but using them as a stone quarry for his barns and byres and outhouses, he built for himself a grand new house of brick – the house you see now.'

He waved his hand in the direction of the house and was silent. Severe, imposing, almost menacing, Crome loomed down on them.

'The great thing about Crome,' said Mr Scogan, seizing the opportunity to speak, 'is the fact that it's so unmistakably and aggressively a work of art. It makes no compromise with nature, but affronts it and rebels against it. It has no likeness to Shelley's tower, in the "Epipsychidion," which, if I remember rightly—

    ' "Seems not now a work of human art,
      But as it were titanic, in the heart
      Of earth having assumed its form and grown
      Out of the mountain, from the living stone,
      Lifting itself in caverns light and high."

No, no; there isn't any nonsense of that sort about Crome. That the hovels of the peasantry should look as though they had grown out of the earth, to which their inmates are attached, is right, no doubt, and suitable. But the house of an intelligent, civilized, and sophisticated man should never seem to have sprouted from the clods. It should rather be an expression of his grand unnatural remoteness from the cloddish life. Since the days of William Morris that's a fact which we in England have been unable to comprehend. Civilized and sophisticated men have solemnly played at being peasants. Hence quaintness, arts and crafts, cottage architecture, and all the rest of it. In the suburbs of our cities you may see, reduplicated in endless rows, studiedly quaint imitations and adaptations of the village hovel. Poverty, ignorance, and a limited range of materials produced the hovel, which possesses undoubtedly, in suitable surroundings, its own "as it were titanic" charm. We now employ our wealth, our technical knowledge, our rich variety of materials for the purpose of building millions of imitation hovels in totally unsuitable surroundings. Could imbecility go further?'

Henry Wimbush took up the thread of his interrupted discourse. 'All that you say, my dear Scogan,' he began, 'is certainly very just, very true. But whether Sir Ferdinando shared your views about architecture or if, indeed, he had any views about architecture at all, I very much doubt. In building this house, Sir Ferdinando was, as a matter of fact, preoccupied by only one thought – the proper placing of his privies. Sanitation was the one great interest of his life. In 1573 he even published, on this subject, a little book – now extremely scarce – called, *Certaine Priuy Counsels* by *One of Her Maiestie's Most Honourable Priuy Counsel, F. L. Knight*, in which the whole matter is treated with great learning and elegance. His guiding principle in arranging the sanitation of a house was to secure that the greatest possible distance should separate the privy from the sewage arrangements. Hence it followed inevitably that the privies were to be placed at the top of the house, being connected by vertical shafts with pits or channels in the ground. It must not be thought that Sir Ferdinando was moved only by material and merely sanitary considerations; for the placing of his privies in an exalted position he had also certain excellent spiritual reasons. For, he argues in the third chapter of his *Priuy Counsels*, the necessities of nature are so base and brutish that in obeying them we are apt to forget that we are the noblest creatures of the universe. To counteract these degrading effects he advised that the privy should be in every house the room nearest to heaven, that it should be well provided with windows commanding an extensive and noble prospect, and that the walls of the chamber should be lined with bookshelves containing all the ripest products of human wisdom, such as the Proverbs of Solomon, Boëthius's *Consolations of Philosophy*, the apophthegms of Epictetus and Marcus Aurelius, the *Enchiridion* of Erasmus, and all other works, ancient or modern, which testify to the nobility of the human soul. In Crome he was able to put his theories into practice. At the top of each of the three projecting towers he placed a privy. From these a shaft went down the whole height of the house, that is to say, more than seventy feet, through the cellars, and into a series of conduits provided with flowing water tunnelled in the ground on a level with the base of the raised terrace. These conduits emptied themselves into the stream several hundred yards below the fish-pond. The total depth of the shafts from the top of the towers to their subterranean conduits was a hundred and two feet. The eighteenth century, with its passion for modernization, swept away these monuments of sanitary ingenuity. Were it not for tradition and the explicit account of them left by Sir Ferdinando, we should be unaware that these noble privies had ever existed. We should even suppose that Sir Ferdinando built this house after this strange and splendid model for merely aesthetic reasons.'

The contemplation of the glories of the past always evoked in Henry Wimbush a certain enthusiasm. Under the grey bowler his face worked and glowed as he spoke. The thought of these vanished privies moved him profoundly. He ceased to speak; the light gradually died out of his face, and it became once more the replica of the grave, polite hat which shaded it. There was a long silence; the same gently melancholy thoughts seemed to possess the mind of each of them. Permanence, transience – Sir Ferdinando and his privies were gone, Crome still stood. How brightly the sun shone and how inevitable was death! The ways of God were strange; the ways of man were stranger still. . . .

'It does one's heart good,' exclaimed Mr Scogan at last, 'to hear of these fantastic English aristocrats. To have a theory about privies and to build an immense and splendid house in order to put it into practice – it's magnificent, beautiful! I like to think of them all : the eccentric milords rolling across Europe in ponderous carriages, bound on extraordinary errands. One is going to Venice to buy La Bianchi's larynx; he won't get it till she's dead, of course, but no matter; he's prepared to wait; he has a collection, pickled in glass bottles, of the throats of famous opera singers. And the instruments of renowned virtuosi – he goes in for them too; he will try to bribe Paganini to part with his little Guarnerio, but he has small hope of success. Paganini won't sell his fiddle; but perhaps he might sacrifice one of his guitars. Others are bound on crusades – one to die miserably among the savage Greeks, another, in his white top hat, to lead Italians against their oppressors. Others have no business at all; they are just giving their oddity a continental airing. At home they cultivate themselves at leisure and with greater elaboration. Beckford builds towers, Portland digs holes in the ground, Cavendish, the millionaire, lives in a stable, eats nothing but

mutton, and amuses himself – oh, solely for his private delec-
tation – by anticipating the electrical discoveries of half a
century. Glorious eccentrics! Every age is enlivened by their
presence. Some day, my dear Denis,' said Mr Scogan, turning a beady bright regard in his direction – 'some day you
must become their biographer – "The Lives of Queer Men."
What a subject! I should like to undertake it myself.'

Mr Scogan paused, looked up once more at the towering
house, then murmured the word, 'Eccentricity,' two or three
times.

'Eccentricity. . . . It's the justification of all aristocracies.
It justifies leisured classes and inherited wealth and privilege
and endowments and all the other injustices of that sort. If
you're to do anything reasonable in this world, you must have
a class of people who are secure, safe from public opinion,
safe from poverty, leisured, not compelled to waste their
time in the imbecile routines that go by the name of Honest
Work. You must have a class of which the members can think
and, within the obvious limits, do what they please. You
must have a class in which people who have eccentricities can
indulge them and in which eccentricity in general will be
tolerated and understood. That's the important thing about
an aristocracy. Not only is it eccentric itself – often grand-
iosely so; it also tolerates and even encourages eccentricity
in others. The eccentricities of the artist and the newfangled
thinker don't inspire it with that fear, loathing, and disgust
which the burgesses instinctively feel towards them. It is a
sort of Red Indian Reservation planted in the midst of a
vast horde of Poor Whites – colonials at that. Within its
boundaries wild men disport themselves – often, it must be
admitted, a little grossly, a little too flamboyantly; and when
kindred spirits are born outside the pale it offers them some
sort of refuge from the hatred which the Poor Whites, *en
bons bourgeois*, lavish on anything that is wild or out of the
ordinary. After the social revolution there will be no Reser-
vations; the Redskins will be drowned in the great sea of Poor
Whites. What then? Will they suffer you to go on writing
villanelles, my good Denis? Will you, unhappy Henry, be
allowed to live in this house of the splendid privies, to continue your quiet delving in the mines of futile knowledge?
Will Anne . . .'

'And you,' said Anne, interrupting him, 'will you be allowed to go on talking?'

'You may rest assured,' Mr Scogan replied, 'that I shall not. I shall have some Honest Work to do.'

CHAPTER XII

'Blight, Mildew, and Smut. . . .' Mary was puzzled and distressed. Perhaps her ears had played her false. Perhaps what
he had really said was, 'Squire, Binyon, and Shanks,' or
'Childe, Blunden, and Earp,' or even 'Abercrombie, Drink-
water, and Rabindranath Tagore.' Perhaps. But then her
ears never did play her false. 'Blight, Mildew, and Smut.'
The impression was distinct and ineffaceable. 'Blight, Mildew . . .' she was forced to the conclusion, reluctantly, that
Denis had indeed pronounced those improbable words. He
had deliberately repelled her attempt to open a serious discussion. That was horrible. A man who would not talk
seriously to a woman just because she was a woman – oh,
impossible! Egeria or nothing. Perhaps Gombauld would be
more satisfactory. True, his meridional heredity was a little
disquieting; but at least he was a serious worker, and it was
with his work that she would associate herself. And Denis?
After all, what *was* Denis? A dilettante, an amateur. . . .

Gombauld had annexed for his painting-room a little
disused granary that stood by itself in a green close beyond
the farmyard. It was a square brick building with a peaked
roof and little windows set high up in each of its walls. A
ladder of four rungs led up to the door; for the granary was
perched above the ground, and out of reach of the rats, on
four massive toadstools of grey stone. Within, there lingered
a faint smell of dust and cobwebs; and the narrow shaft of
sunlight that came slanting in at every hour of the day
through one of the little windows was always alive with
silvery motes. Here Gombauld worked, with a kind of con-
centrated ferocity, during six or seven hours of each day.
He was pursuing something new, something terrific, if only
he could catch it.

During the last eight years, nearly half of which had been
spent in the process of winning the war, he had worked his
way industriously through cubism. Now he had come out on
the other side. He had begun by painting a formalized
nature; then, little by little, he had risen from nature into

the world of pure form, till in the end he was painting nothing but his own thoughts, externalized in the abstract geometrical forms of the mind's devising. He found the process arduous and exhilarating. And then, quite suddenly, he grew dissatisfied; he felt himself cramped and confined within intolerably narrow limitations. He was humiliated to find how few and crude and uninteresting were the forms he could invent; the inventions of nature were without number, inconceivably subtle and elaborate. He had done with cubism. He was out on the other side. But the cubist discipline preserved him from falling into excesses of nature worship. He took from nature its rich, subtle, elaborate forms, but his aim was always to work them into a whole that should have the thrilling simplicity and formality of an idea; to combine prodigious realism with prodigious simplification. Memories of Caravaggio's portentous achievements haunted him. Forms of a breathing, living reality emerged from darkness, built themselves up into compositions as luminously simple and single as a mathematical idea. He thought of the 'Call of Matthew,' of 'Peter Crucified,' of the 'Lute Players,' of 'Magdalen.' He had the secret, that astonishing ruffian, he had the secret! And now Gombauld was after it, in hot pursuit. Yes, it would be something terrific, if only he could catch it.

For a long time an idea had been stirring and spreading, yeastily, in his mind. He had made a portfolio full of studies, he had drawn a cartoon; and now the idea was taking shape on canvas. A man fallen from a horse. The huge animal, a gaunt white cart-horse, filled the upper half of the picture with its great body. Its head, lowered towards the ground, was in shadow; the immense bony body was what arrested the eye, the body and the legs, which came down on either side of the picture like the pillars of an arch. On the ground, between the legs of the towering beast, lay the foreshortened figure of a man, the head in the extreme foreground, the arms flung wide to right and left. A white, relentless light poured down from a point in the right foreground. The beast, the fallen man, were sharply illuminated; round them, beyond and behind them, was the night. They were alone in the darkness, a universe in themselves. The horse's body filled the upper part of the picture; the legs, the great hoofs, frozen to stillness in the midst of their trampling, limited it on either side. And beneath lay the man, his foreshortened face at the focal point in the centre, his arms outstretched towards the sides of the picture. Under the arch of the horse's belly, between his legs, the eye looked through into an intense darkness; below, the space was closed in by the figure of the prostrate man. A central gulf of darkness surrounded by luminous forms. . . .

The picture was more than half finished. Gombauld had been at work all the morning on the figure of the man, and now he was taking a rest – the time to smoke a cigarette. Tilting back his chair till it touched the wall, he looked thoughtfully at his canvas. He was pleased, and at the same time he was desolated. In itself, the thing was good; he knew it. But that something he was after, that something that would be so terrific if only he could catch it – had he caught it? Would he ever catch it?

Three little taps – rat, tat, tat! Surprised, Gombauld turned his eyes towards the door. Nobody ever disturbed him while he was at work; it was one of the unwritten laws. 'Come in!' he called. The door, which was ajar, swung open, revealing, from the waist upwards, the form of Mary. She had only dared to mount half-way up the ladder. If he didn't want her, retreat would be easier and more dignified than if she climbed to the top.

'May I come in?' she asked.

'Certainly.'

She skipped up the remaining two rungs and was over the threshold in an instant. 'A letter came for you by the second post,' she said. 'I thought it might be important, so I brought it out to you.' Her eyes, her childish face were luminously candid as she handed him the letter. There had never been a flimsier pretext.

Gombauld looked at the envelope and put it in his pocket unopened. 'Luckily,' he said, 'it isn't at all important. Thanks very much all the same.'

There was a silence; Mary felt a little uncomfortable. 'May I have a look at what you've been painting?' she had the courage to say at last.

Gombauld had only half smoked his cigarette; in any case he wouldn't begin work again till he had finished. He would give her the five minutes that separated him from the bitter end. 'This is the best place to see it from,' he said.

Mary looked at the picture for some time without saying anything. Indeed, she didn't know what to say; she was taken aback, she was at a loss. She had expected a cubist masterpiece, and here was a picture of a man and a horse, not only recognizable as such, but even aggressively in drawing. *Trompe-l'œil* – there was no other word to describe the delineation of that foreshortened figure under the trampling feet of the horse. What was she to think, what was she to say? Her orientations were gone. One could admire representationalism in the Old Masters. Obviously. But in a modern . . .? At eighteen she might have done so. But now, after five years of schooling among the best judges, her instinctive reaction to a contemporary piece of representation was contempt – an outburst of laughing disparagement. What could Gombauld be up to? She had felt so safe in admiring his work before. But now – she didn't know what to think. It was very difficult, very difficult.

'There's rather a lot of chiaroscuro, isn't there?' she ventured at last, and inwardly congratulated herself on having found a critical formula so gentle and at the same time so penetrating.

'There is,' Gombauld agreed.

Mary was pleased; he accepted her criticism; it was a serious discussion. She put her head on one side and screwed up her eyes. 'I think it's awfully fine,' she said. 'But of course it's a little too . . . too . . . *trompe-l'œil* for my taste.' She looked at Gombauld, who made no response, but continued to smoke, gazing meditatively all the time at his picture. Mary went on gaspingly. 'When I was in Paris this spring I saw a lot of Tschuplitski. I admire his work so tremendously. Of course, it's frightfully abstract now – frightfully abstract and frightfully intellectual. He just throws a few oblongs on to his canvas – quite flat, you know, and painted in pure primary colours. But his design is wonderful. He's getting more and more abstract every day. He'd quite given up the third dimension when I was there and was just thinking of giving up the second. Soon, he says, there'll be just the blank canvas. That's the logical conclusion. Complete abstraction. Painting's finished; he's finishing it. When he's reached pure

62

abstraction he's going to take up architecture. He says it's more intellectual than painting. Do you agree?' she asked, with a final gasp.

Gombauld dropped his cigarette end and trod on it. 'Tschuplitski's finished painting,' he said. 'I've finished my cigarette. But I'm going on painting.' And, advancing towards her, he put his arm round her shoulders and turned her round, away from the picture.

Mary looked up at him; her hair swung back, a soundless bell of gold. Her eyes were serene; she smiled. So the moment had come. His arm was round her. He moved slowly, almost imperceptibly, and she moved with him. It was a peripatetic embracement. 'Do you agree with him?' she repeated. The moment might have come, but she would not cease to be intellectual, serious.

'I don't know. I shall have to think about it.' Gombauld loosened his embrace, his hand dropped from her shoulder. 'Be careful going down the ladder,' he added solicitously.

Mary looked round, startled. They were in front of the open door. She remained standing there for a moment in bewilderment. The hand that had rested on her shoulder made itself felt lower down her back; it administered three of four kindly little smacks. Replying automatically to its stimulus, she moved forward.

'Be careful going down the ladder,' said Gombauld once more.

She was careful. The door closed behind her and she was alone in the little green close. She walked slowly back through the farmyard; she was pensive.

CHAPTER XIII

Henry Wimbush brought down with him to dinner a budget
of printed sheets loosely bound together in a cardboard
portfolio.

'Today,' he said, exhibiting it with a certain solemnity,
'today I have finished the printing of my *History of Crome.*
I helped to set up the type of the last page this evening.'

'The famous History?' cried Anne. The writing and the
printing of this *Magnum Opus* had been going on as long as
she could remember. All her childhood long Uncle Henry's
History had been a vague and fabulous thing, often heard of
and never seen.

'It has taken me nearly thirty years,' said Mr Wimbush.
'Twenty-five years of writing and nearly four of printing.
And now it's finished – the whole chronicle, from Sir Ferdinando Lapith's birth to the death of my father William
Wimbush – more than three centuries and a half : a history
of Crome, written at Crome, and printed at Crome by my
own press.'

'Shall we be allowed to read it now it's finished?' asked
Denis.

Mr Wimbush nodded. 'Certainly,' he said. 'And I hope
you will not find it uninteresting,' he added modestly. 'Our
muniment room is particularly rich in ancient records, and
I have some genuinely new light to throw on the introduction
of the three-pronged fork.'

'And the people?' asked Gombauld. 'Sir Ferdinando and
the rest of them – were they amusing? Were there any crimes
or tragedies in the family?'

'Let me see,' Henry Wimbush rubbed his chin thoughtfully. 'I can only think of two suicides, one violent death,
four or perhaps five broken hearts, and half a dozen little
blots on the scutcheon in the way of misalliances, seductions,
natural children, and the like. No, on the whole, it's a placid
and uneventful record.'

'The Wimbushes and the Lapiths were always an un-
adventurous, respectable crew,' said Priscilla, with a note of

scorn in her voice. 'If I were to write my family history now!
Why, it would be one long continuous blot from beginning
to end.' She laughed jovially, and helped herself to another
glass of wine.

'If I were to write mine,' Mr Scogan remarked, 'it wouldn't
exist. After the second generation we Scogans are lost in the
mists of antiquity.'

'After dinner,' said Henry Wimbush, a little piqued by his
wife's disparaging comment on the masters of Crome, 'I'll
read you an episode from my History that will make you
admit that even the Lapiths, in their own respectable way,
had their tragedies and strange adventures.'

'I'm glad to hear it,' said Priscilla.

'Glad to hear what?' asked Jenny, emerging suddenly
from her private interior world like a cuckoo from a clock.
She received an explanation, smiled, nodded, cuckooed a
last 'I see,' and popped back, clapping shut the door behind
her.

Dinner was eaten; the party had adjourned to the drawing-room.

'Now,' said Henry Wimbush, pulling up a chair to the
lamp. He put on his round pince-nez, rimmed with tortoise-
shell, and began cautiously to turn over the pages of his loose
and still fragmentary book. He found his place at last. 'Shall
I begin?' he asked, looking up.

'Do,' said Priscilla, yawning.

In the midst of an attentive silence Mr Wimbush gave a
little preliminary cough and started to read.

'The infant who was destined to become the fourth baronet
of the name of Lapith was born in the year 1740. He was a
very small baby, weighing not more than three pounds at
birth, but from the first he was sturdy and healthy. In honour
of his maternal grandfather, Sir Hercules Occam of Bishop's
Occam, he was christened Hercules. His mother, like many
other mothers, kept a notebook, in which his progress from
month to month was recorded. He walked at ten months, and
before his second year was out he had learnt to speak a number of words. At three years he weighed but twenty-four
pounds, and at six, though he could read and write perfectly
and showed a remarkable aptitude for music, he was no
larger and heavier than a well-grown child of two.

Meanwhile, his mother had borne two other children, a boy and a girl, one of whom died of croup during infancy, while the other was carried off by smallpox before it reached the age of five. Hercules remained the only surviving child.

'On his twelfth birthday Hercules was still only three feet and two inches in height. His head, which was very handsome and nobly shaped, was too big for his body, but otherwise he was exquisitely proportioned and, for his size, of great strength and agility. His parents, in the hope of making him grow, consulted all the most eminent physicians of the time. Their various prescriptions were followed to the letter, but in vain. One ordered a very plentiful meat diet; another exercise; a third constructed a little rack, modelled on those employed by the Holy Inquisition, on which young Hercules was stretched, with excruciating torments, for half an hour every morning and evening. In the course of the next three years Hercules gained perhaps two inches. After that his growth stopped completely, and he remained for the rest of his life a pigmy of three feet and four inches. His father, who had built the most extravagant hopes upon his son, planning for him in his imagination a military career equal to that of Marlborough, found himself a disappointed man. "I have brought an abortion into the world," he would say, and he took so violent a dislike to his son that the boy dared scarcely come into his presence. His temper, which had been serene, was turned by disappointment to moroseness and savagery. He avoided all company (being, as he said, ashamed to show himself, the father of a *lusus naturae*, among normal, healthy human beings), and took to solitary drinking, which carried him very rapidly to his grave; for the year before Hercules came of age his father was taken off by an apoplexy. His mother, whose love for him had increased with the growth of his father's unkindness, did not long survive, but little more than a year after her husband's death succumbed, after eating two dozen of oysters, to an attack of typhoid fever.

'Hercules thus found himself at the age of twenty-one alone in the world, and master of a considerable fortune, including the estate and mansion of Crome. The beauty and intelligence of his childhood had survived into his manly age, and, but for his dwarfish stature, he would have taken his place among the handsomest and most accomplished young men of his time. He was well read in Greek and Latin authors, as well as in all the moderns of any merit who had written in English, French, or Italian. He had a good ear for music, and was no indifferent performer on the violin, which he used to play like a bass viol, seated on a chair with the instrument between his legs. To the music of the harpsichord and clavichord he was extremely partial, but the smallness of his hands made it impossible for him ever to perform upon these instruments. He had a small ivory flute made for him, on which, whenever he was melancholy, he used to play a simple country air or jig, affirming that this rustic music had more power to clear and raise the spirits than the most artificial productions of the masters. From an early age he practised the composition of poetry, but, though conscious of his great powers in this art, he would never publish any specimen of his writing. "My stature," he would say, "is reflected in my verses; if the public were to read them it would not be because I am a poet, but because I am a dwarf." Several MS books of Sir Hercules's poems survive. A single specimen will suffice to illustrate his qualities as a poet.

"In ancient days, while yet the world was young,
  Ere Abram fed his flocks or Homer sung;
  When blacksmith Tubal tamed creative fire,
  And Jabal dwelt in tents and Jubal struck the lyre;
  Flesh grown corrupt brought forth a monstrous birth
  And obscene giants trod the shrinking earth,
  Till God, impatient of their sinful brood,
  Gave rein to wrath and drown'd them in the Flood.
  Teeming again, repeopled Tellus bore
  The lubber Hero and the Man of War;
  Huge towers of Brawn, topp'd with an empty Skull,
  Witlessly bold, heroically dull.
  Long ages pass'd and Man grown more refin'd,
  Slighter in muscle but of vaster Mind,
  Smiled at his grandsire's broadsword, bow and bill,
  And learn'd to wield the Pencil and the Quill.
  The glowing canvas and the written page

Immortaliz'd his name from age to age,
His name emblazon'd on Fame's temple wall;
For Art grew great as Humankind grew small.
Thus man's long progress step by step we trace;
The Giant dies, the hero takes his place;
The Giant vile, the dull heroic Block :
At one we shudder and at one we mock.
Man last appears. In him the Soul's pure flame
Burns brightlier in a not inord'nate frame.
Of old when Heroes fought and Giants swarmed,
Men were huge mounds of matter scarce inform'd;
Wearied by leavening so vast a mass,
The spirit slept and all the mind was crass.
The smaller carcase of these later days
Is soon inform'd; the Soul unwearied plays
And like a Pharos darts abroad her mental rays.
But can we think that Providence will stay
Man's footsteps here upon the upward way?
Mankind in understanding and in grace
Advanc'd so far beyond the Giants' race?
Hence impious thought ! Still led by GOD's own Hand,
Mankind proceeds towards the Promised Land.
A time will come (prophetic, I descry
Remoter dawns along the gloomy sky),
When happy mortals of a Golden Age
Will backward turn the dark historic page,
And in our vaunted race of Men behold
A form as gross, a Mind as dead and cold,
As we in Giants see, in warriors of old.
A time will come, wherein the soul shall be
From all superfluous matter wholly free :
When the light body, agile as a fawn's,
Shall sport with grace along the velvet lawns.
Nature's most delicate and final birth,
Mankind perfected shall possess the earth.
But ah, not yet ! For still the Giants' race,
Huge, though diminish'd, tramps the Earth's fair face;
Gross and repulsive, yet perversely proud,
Men of their imperfections boast aloud.
Vain of their bulk, of all they still retain
Of giant ugliness absurdly vain;

At all that's small they point their stupid scorn
And, monsters, think themselves divinely born.
Sad is the Fate of those, ah, sad indeed,
The rare precursors of the nobler breed!
Who come man's golden glory to foretell,
But pointing Heav'nwards live themselves in Hell.

'As soon as he came into the estate, Sir Hercules set about remodelling his household. For though by no means ashamed of his deformity – indeed, if we may judge from the poem quoted above, he regarded himself as being in many ways superior to the ordinary race of man – he found the presence of full-grown men and women embarrassing. Realizing, too, that he must abandon all ambitions in the great world, he determined to retire absolutely from it and to create, as it were, at Crome a private world of his own, in which all should be proportionable to himself. Accordingly, he discharged all the old servants of the house and replaced them gradually, as he was able to find suitable successors, by others of dwarfish stature. In the course of a few years he had assembled about himself a numerous household, no member of which was above four feet high and the smallest among them scarcely two feet and six inches. His father's dogs, such as setters, mastiffs, greyhounds, and a pack of beagles, he sold or gave away as too large and too boisterous for his house, replacing them by pugs and King Charles spaniels and whatever other breeds of dog were the smallest. His father's stable was also sold. For his own use, whether riding or driving, he had six black Shetland ponies, with four very choice piebald animals of New Forest breed.

'Having thus settled his household entirely to his own satisfaction, it only remained for him to find some suitable companion with whom to share this paradise. Sir Hercules had a susceptible heart, and had more than once, between the ages of sixteen and twenty, felt what it was to love. But here his deformity had been a source of the most bitter humiliation, for, having once dared to declare himself to a young lady of his choice, he had been received with laughter. On his persisting, she had picked him up and shaken him like an importunate child, telling him to run away and plague her no more. The story soon got about – indeed, the young

lady herself used to tell it as a particularly pleasant anecdote
– and the taunts and mockery it occasioned were a source of
the most acute distress to Hercules. From the poems written
at this period we gather that he meditated taking his own life.
In course of time, however, he lived down this humiliation;
but never again, though he often fell in love, and that very
passionately, did he dare to make any advances to those in
whom he was interested. After coming to the estate and
finding that he was in a position to create his own world as
he desired it, he saw that, if he was to have a wife – which
he very much desired, being of an affectionate and, indeed,
amorous temper – he must choose her as he had chosen his
servants – from among the race of dwarfs. But to find a
suitable wife was, he found, a matter of some difficulty; for
he would marry none who was not distinguished by beauty
and gentle birth. The dwarfish daughter of Lord Bemboro
he refused on the ground that besides being a pigmy she was
hunchbacked; while another young lady, an orphan belong-
ing to a very good family in Hampshire, was rejected by
him because her face, like that of so many dwarfs
wizened and repulsive. Finally, when he was almost des-
pairing of success, he heard from a reliable source that Count
Titimalo, a Venetian nobleman, possessed a daughter of
exquisite beauty and great accomplishments, who was but
three feet in height. Setting out at once for Venice, he went
immediately on his arrival to pay his respects to the count,
whom he found living with his wife and five children in a
very mean apartment in one of the poorer quarters of the
town. Indeed, the count was so far reduced in his circumstances that he was even then negotiating (so it was
rumoured) with a travelling company of clowns and acro-
bats, who had had the misfortune to lose their performing
dwarf, for the sale of his diminutive daughter Filomena. Sir
Hercules arrived in time to save her from this untoward fate,
for he was so much charmed by Filomena's grace and beauty,
that at the end of three days' courtship he made her a formal
offer of marriage, which was accepted by her no less joyfully
than by her father, who perceived in an English son-in-law
a rich and unfailing source of revenue. After an unostenta-
tious marriage, at which the English ambassador acted as
one of the witnesses, Sir Hercules and his bride returned by

sea to England, where they settled down, as it proved, to a life of uneventful happiness.

'Crome and its household of dwarfs delighted Filomena, who felt herself now for the first time to be a free woman living among her equals in a friendly world. She had many tastes in common with her husband, especially that of music. She had a beautiful voice, of a power surprising in one so small, and could touch A in alt without effort. Accompanied by her husband on his fine Cremona fiddle, which he played, as we have noted before, as one plays a bass viol, she would sing all the liveliest and tenderest airs from the operas and cantatas of her native country. Seated together at the harpsichord, they found that they could with their four hands play all the music written for two hands of ordinary size, a circumstance which gave Sir Hercules unfailing pleasure.

'When they were not making music or reading together, which they often did, both in English and Italian, they spent their time in healthful outdoor exercises, sometimes rowing in a little boat on the lake, but more often riding or driving, occupations in which, because they were entirely new to her, Filomena especially delighted. When she had become a perfectly proficient rider, Filomena and her husband used often to go hunting in the park, at that time very much more extensive than it is now. They hunted no foxes nor hares, but rabbits, using a pack of about thirty black and fawn-coloured pugs, a kind of dog which, when not overfed, can course a rabbit as well as any of the smaller breeds. Four dwarf grooms, dressed in scarlet liveries and mounted on white Exmoor ponies, hunted the pack, while their master and mistress, in green habits, followed either on the black Shetlands or on the piebald New Forest ponies. A picture of the whole hunt – dogs, horses, grooms, and masters – was painted by William Stubbs, whose work Sir Hercules admired so much that he invited him, though a man of ordinary stature, to come and stay at the mansion for the purpose of executing this picture. Stubbs likewise painted a portrait of Sir Hercules and his lady driving in their green enamelled calash drawn by four black Shetlands. Sir Hercules wears a plum-coloured velvet coat and white breeches; Filomena is dressed in flowered muslin and a very large hat with pink feathers. The two figures in their gay carriage stand out sharply against a dark background of trees; but to the left of the picture the trees fall away and disappear, so that the four black ponies are seen against a pale and strangely lurid sky that has the golden-brown colour of thunder-clouds lighted up by the sun.

'In this way four years passed happily by. At the end of that time Filomena found herself great with child. Sir Hercules was overjoyed. "If God is good," he wrote in his day-book, "the name of Lapith will be preserved and our rarer and more delicate race transmitted through the generations until in the fullness of time the world shall recognize the superiority of those beings whom now it uses to make mock of." On his wife's being brought to bed of a son he wrote a poem to the same effect. The child was christened Ferdinando in memory of the builder of the house.

'With the passage of the months a certain sense of disquiet began to invade the minds of Sir Hercules and his lady. For the child was growing with an extraordinary rapidity. At a year he weighed as much as Hercules had weighed when he was three. "Ferdinando goes *crescendo*," wrote Filomena in her diary. "It seems not natural." At eighteen months the baby was almost as tall as their smallest jockey, who was a man of thirty-six. Could it be that Ferdinando was destined to become a man of the normal, gigantic dimensions? It was a thought to which neither of his parents dared yet give open utterance, but in the secrecy of their respective diaries they brooded over it in terror and dismay.

'On his third birthday Ferdinando was taller than his mother and not more than a couple of inches short of his father's height. "Today for the first time," wrote Sir Hercules, "we discussed the situation. The hideous truth can be concealed no longer : Ferdinando is not one of us. On this, his third birthday, a day when we should have been rejoicing at the health, the strength, and beauty of our child, we wept together over the ruin of our happiness. God give us strength to bear this cross."

'At the age of eight Ferdinando was so large and so exuberantly healthy that his parents decided, though reluctantly, to send him to school. He was packed off to Eton at the beginning of the next half. A profound peace settled upon the house. Ferdinando returned for the summer holidays larger and stronger than ever. One day he knocked down the butler and broke his arm. "He is rough, inconsiderate, unamenable to persuasion," wrote his father. "The only thing that will teach him manners is corporal chastisement." Ferdinando, who at this age was already seventeen inches taller than his father, received no corporal chastisement.

'One summer holidays about three years later Ferdinando returned to Crome accompanied by a very large mastiff dog. He had bought it from an old man at Windsor who found the beast too expensive to feed. It was a savage, unreliable animal; hardly had it entered the house when it attacked one of Sir Hercules's favourite pugs, seizing the creature in its jaws and shaking it till it was nearly dead. Extremely put out by this occurrence, Sir Hercules ordered that the beast should be chained up in the stable-yard. Ferdinando sullenly answered that the dog was his, and he would keep it where he pleased. His father, growing angry, bade him take the animal out of the house at once, on pain of his utmost displeasure. Ferdinando refused to move. His mother at this moment coming into the room, the dog flew at her, knocked her down, and in a twinkling had very severely mauled her arm and shoulder; in another instant it must infallibly have had her by the throat, had not Sir Hercules drawn his sword and stabbed the animal to the heart. Turning on his son, he ordered him to leave the room immediately, as being unfit to remain in the same place with the mother whom he had nearly murdered. So awe-inspiring was the spectacle of Sir Hercules standing with one foot on the carcase of the gigantic dog, his sword drawn and still bloody, so commanding were his voice, his gestures, and the expression of his face, that Ferdinando slunk out of the room in terror and behaved himself for all the rest of the vacation in an entirely exemplary fashion. His mother soon recovered from the bites of the mastiff, but the effect on her mind of this adventure was ineradicable; from that time forth she lived always among imaginary terrors.

'The two years which Ferdinando spent on the Continent, making the Grand Tour, were a period of happy repose for his parents. But even now the thought of the future haunted them; nor were they able to solace themselves with all the diversions of their younger days. The Lady Filomena had

73

lost her voice and Sir Hercules was grown too rheumatical to play the violin. He, it is true, still rode after his pugs, but his wife felt herself too old and, since the episode of the mastiff, too nervous for such sports. At most, to please her husband, she would follow the hunt at a distance in a little gig drawn by the safest and oldest of the Shetlands.

'The day fixed for Ferdinando's return came round. Filomena, sick with vague dreads and presentiments, retired to her chamber and her bed. Sir Hercules received his son alone. A giant in a brown travelling-suit entered the room. "Welcome home, my son," said Sir Hercules in a voice that trembled a little.

' "I hope I see you well, sir." Ferdinando bent down to shake hands, then straightened himself up again. The top of his father's head reached to the level of his hip.

'Ferdinando had not come alone. Two friends of his own age accompanied him, and each of the young men had brought a servant. Not for thirty years had Crome been desecrated by the presence of so many members of the common race of men. Sir Hercules was appalled and indignant, but the laws of hospitality had to be obeyed. He received the young gentlemen with grave politeness and sent the servants to the kitchen, with orders that they should be well cared for.

'The old family dining-table was dragged out into the light and dusted (Sir Hercules and his lady were accustomed to dine at a small table twenty inches high). Simon, the aged butler, who could only just look over the edge of the big table, was helped at supper by the three servants brought by Ferdinando and his guests.

'Sir Hercules presided, and with his usual grace supported a conversation on the pleasures of foreign travel, the beauties of art and nature to be met with abroad, the opera at Venice, the singing of the orphans in the churches of the same city, and on other topics of a similar nature. The young men were not particularly attentive to his discourses; they were occupied in watching the efforts of the butler to change the plates and replenish the glasses. They covered their laughter by violent and repeated fits of coughing or choking. Sir Hercules affected not to notice, but changed the subject of the conversation to sport. Upon this one of the young men asked

74

whether it was true, as he had heard, that he used to hunt the rabbit with a pack of pug dogs. Sir Hercules replied that it was, and proceeded to describe the chase in some detail. The young men roared with laughter.

'When supper was over, Sr Hercules climbed down from his chair and, giving as his excuse that he must see how his lady did, bade them good-night. The sound of laughter followed him up the stairs. Filomena was not asleep; she had been lying on her bed listening to the sound of enormous laughter and the tread of strangely heavy feet on the stairs and along the corridors. Sir Hercules drew a chair to her bedside and sat there for a long time in silence, holding his wife's hand and sometimes gently squeezing it. At about ten o'clock they were startled by a violent noise. There was a breaking of glass, a stamping of feet, with an outburst of shouts and laughter. The uproar continuing for several minutes, Sir Hercules rose to his feet and, in spite of his wife's entreaties, prepared to go and see what was happening. There was no light on the staircase, and Sir Hercules groped his way down cautiously, lowering himself from stair to stair and standing for a moment on each tread before adventuring on a new step. The noise was louder here; the shouting articulated itself into recognizable words and phrases. A line of light was visible under the dining-room door. Sir Hercules tiptoed across the hall towards it. Just as he approached the door there was another terrific crash of breaking glass and jangled metal. What could they be doing? Standing on tiptoe he managed to look through the keyhole. In the middle of the ravaged table old Simon, the butler, so primed with drink that he could scarcely keep his balance, was dancing a jig. His feet crunched and tinkled among the broken glass, and his shoes were wet with spilt wine. The three young men sat round, thumping the table with their hands or with the empty wine bottles, shouting and laughing encouragement. The three servants leaning against the wall laughed too. Ferdinando suddenly threw a handful of walnuts at the dancer's head, which so dazed and surprised the little man that he staggered and fell down on his back, upsetting a decanter and several glasses. They raised him up, gave him some brandy to drink, thumped him on the back. The old man smiled and hiccoughed, "Tomorrow," said Ferdinando,

"we'll have a concerted ballet of the whole household."
"With father Hercules wearing his club and lion-skin," added
one of his companions, and all three roared with laughter.

'Sir Hercules would look and listen no further. He crossed
the hall once more and began to climb the stairs, lifting his
knees painfully high at each degree. This was the end; there
was no place for him now in the world, no place for him and
Ferdinando together.

'His wife was still awake; to her questioning glance he
answered, "They are making mock of old Simon. Tomorrow
it will be our turn." They were silent for a time.

'At last Filomena said, "I do not want to see tomorrow."

' "It is better not," said Sir Hercules. Going into his closet
he wrote in his day-book a full and particular account of all
the events of the evening. While he was still engaged in this
task he rang for a servant and ordered hot water and a bath
to be made ready for him at eleven o'clock. When he had
finished writing he went into his wife's room, and preparing
a dose of opium twenty times as strong as that which she was
accustomed to take when she could not sleep, he brought it
to her, saying, "Here is your sleeping-draught."

'Filomena took the glass and lay for a little time, but did
not drink immediately. The tears came into her eyes. "Do you
remember the songs we used to sing, sitting out there *sulla
terrazza* in summer-time?" She began singing softly in her
ghost of a cracked voice a few bars from Stradella's "*Amor,
amor, non dormir piu.*" "And you playing on the violin. It
seems such a short time ago, and yet so long, long, long.
Addio, amore. A rivederti." She drank off the draught and,
lying back on the pillow, closed her eyes. Sir Hercules kissed
her hand and tiptoed away, as though he were afraid of
waking her. He returned to his closet, and having recorded
his wife's last words to him, he poured into his bath the water
that had been brought up in accordance with his orders.
The water being too hot for him to get into the bath at once,
he took down from the shelf his copy of Suetonius. He wished
to read how Seneca had died. He opened the book at ran-
dom. "But dwarfs," he read, "he held in abhorrence as being
lusus naturae and of evil omen." He winced as though he
had been struck. This same Augustus, he remembered, had
exhibited in the amphitheatre a young man called Lucius, of

good family, who was not quite two feet in height and weighed seventeen pounds, but had a stentorian voice. He turned over the pages. Tiberius, Caligula, Claudius, Nero : it was a tale of growing horror. "Seneca his preceptor, he forced to kill himself." And there was Petronius, who had called his friends about him at the last, bidding them talk to him, not of the consolations of philosophy, but of love and gallantry, while the life was ebbing away through his opened veins. Dipping his pen once more in the ink he wrote on the last page of his diary : "He died a Roman death." Then, putting the toes of one foot into the water and finding that it was not too hot, he threw off his dressing-gown and, taking a razor in his hand, sat down in the bath. With one deep cut he severed the artery in his left wrist, then lay back and composed his mind to meditation. The blood oozed out, floating through the water in dissolving wreaths and spirals. In a little while the whole bath was tinged with pink. The colour deepened; Sir Hercules felt himself mastered by an invincible drowsiness; he was sinking from vague dream to dream. Soon he was sound asleep. There was not much blood in his small body.'

CHAPTER XIV

For their after-luncheon coffee the party generally adjourned to the library. Its windows looked east, and at this hour of the day it was the coolest place in the whole house. It was a large room, fitted, during the eighteenth century, with white painted shelves of an elegant design. In the middle of one wall a door, ingeniously upholstered with rows of dummy books, gave access to a deep cupboard, where, among a pile of letter-files and old newspapers, the mummy-case of an Egyptian lady, brought back by the second Sir Ferdinando on his return from the Grand Tour, mouldered in the darkness. From ten yards away and at a first glance, one might almost have mistaken this secret door for a section of shelving filled with genuine books. Coffee-cup in hand, Mr Scogan was standing in front of the dummy book-shelf. Between the sips he discoursed.

'The bottom shelf,' he was saying, 'is taken up by an Encyclopaedia in fourteen volumes. Useful, but a little dull, as is also Caprimulge's *Dictionary of the Finnish Language*. The *Biographical Dictionary* looks much more promising. *Biography of Men who were Born Great, Biography of Men who Achieved Greatness, Biography of Men who had Greatness Thrust upon Them,* and *Biography of Men who were Never Great at All.* Then there are ten volumes of *Thom's Works and Wanderings*, while the *Wild Goose Chase, a Novel,* by an anonymous author, fills no less than six. But what's this, what's this?' Mr Scogan stood on tiptoe and peered up. 'Seven volumes of the *Tales of Knockespotch*. The *Tales of Knockespotch*,' he repeated. 'Ah, my dear Henry,' he said, turning round, 'these are your best books. I would willingly give all the rest of your library for them.'

The happy possessor of a multitude of first editions, Mr Wimbush could afford to smile indulgently.

'Is it possible,' Mr Scogan went on, 'that they possess nothing more than a back and a title?' He opened the cupboard door and peeped inside, as though he hoped to find the rest of the books behind it. 'Phooh!' he said, and shut the door again. 'It smells of dust and mildew. How symbolical! One comes to the great masterpieces of the past, expecting some miraculous illumination, and one finds, on opening them, only darkness and dust and a faint smell of decay. After all, what is reading but a vice, like drink or venery or any other form of excessive self-indulgence? One reads to tickle and amuse one's mind; one reads, above all, to prevent oneself thinking. Still – the *Tales of Knockespotch* . . .'

He paused, and thoughtfully drummed with his fingers on the backs of the non-existent, unattainable books.

'But I disagree with you about reading,' said Mary. 'About serious reading, I mean.'

'Quite right, Mary, quite right,' Mr Scogan answered. 'I had forgotten there were any serious people in the room.'

'I like the idea of the Biographies,' said Denis. 'There's room for us all within the scheme; it's comprehensive.'

'Yes, the Biographies are good, the Biographies are excellent,' Mr Scogan agreed. 'I imagine them written in a very elegant Regency style – Brighton Pavilion in words – perhaps by the great Dr Lemprière himself. You know his classical dictionary? Ah!' Mr Scogan raised his hand and let it limply fall again in a gesture which implied that words failed him. 'Read his biography of Helen; read how Jupiter, disguised as a swan, was "enabled to avail himself of his situation" *vis-à-vis* to Leda. And to think that he may have, must have written these biographies of the Great! What a work, Henry! And, owing to the idiotic arrangement of your library, it can't be read.'

'I prefer the *Wild Goose Chase*,' said Anne. 'A novel in six volumes – it must be restful.'

'Restful,' Mr Scogan repeated. 'You've hit on the right word. A *Wild Goose Chase* is sound, but a bit old-fashioned – pictures of clerical life in the fifties, you know; specimens of the landed gentry; peasants for pathos and comedy; and in the background, always the picturesque beauties of nature soberly described. All very good and solid, but, like certain puddings, just a little dull. Personally, I like much better the notion of *Thom's Works and Wanderings*. The eccentric Mr Thom of Thom's Hill. Old Tom Thom, as his intimates used to call him. He spent ten years in Tibet organizing the clarified butter industry on modern European lines, and was able to retire at thirty-six with a handsome fortune. The rest of his life he devoted to travel and ratiocination; here is the result.' Mr Scogan tapped the dummy books. 'And now we come to the *Tales of Knockespotch*. What a masterpiece and what a great man! Knockespotch knew how to write fiction. Ah, Denis, if you could only read Knockespotch you wouldn't be writing a novel about the wearisome development of a young man's character, you wouldn't be describing in endless, fastidious detail, cultured life in Chelsea and Bloomsbury and Hampstead. You would be trying to write a readable book. But then, alas! owing to the peculiar arrangement of our host's library, you never will read Knockespotch.'

'Nobody could regret the fact more than I do,' said Denis.

'It was Knockespotch,' Mr Scogan continued, 'the great Knockespotch, who delivered us from the dreary tyranny of the realistic novel. My life, Knockespotch said, is not so long that I can afford to spend precious hours writing or reading descriptions of middle-class interiors. He said again, "I am tired of seeing the human mind bogged in a social plenum; I prefer to paint it in a vacuum, freely and sportively bombinating."'

'I say,' said Gombauld, 'Knockespotch was a little obscure sometimes, wasn't he?'

'He was,' Mr Scogan replied, 'and with intention. It made him seem even profounder than he actually was. But it was only in his aphorisms that he was so dark and oracular. In his Tales he was always luminous. Oh, those Tales – those Tales! How shall I describe them? Fabulous characters shoot across his pages like gaily dressed performers on the trapeze. There are extraordinary adventures and still more extraordinary speculations. Intelligences and emotions, relieved of all the imbecile preoccupations of civilized life, move in intricate and subtle dances, crossing and recrossing, advancing, retreating, impinging. An immense erudition and an immense fancy go hand in hand. All the ideas of the present and of the past, on every possible subject, bob up among the Tales, smile gravely or grimace a caricature of themselves, then disappear to make place for something new. The verbal surface of his writing is rich and fantastically diversified. The wit is incessant. The . . .'

'But couldn't you give us a specimen,' Denis broke in – 'a concrete example?'

'Alas!' Mr Scogan replied, 'Knockespotch's great book is like the sword Excalibur. It remains stuck fast in this door, awaiting the coming of a writer with genius enough to draw it forth. I am not even a writer, I am not so much as qualified to attempt the task. The extraction of Knockespotch from his wooden prison I leave, my dear Denis, to you.'

'Thank you,' said Denis.

CHAPTER XV

'In the time of the amiable Brantôme,' Mr Scogan was saying, 'every debutante at the French Court was invited to
dine at the King's table, where she was served with wine in
a handsome silver cup of Italian workmanship. It was no
ordinary cup, this goblet of the debutantes; for, inside, it had
been most curiously and ingeniously engraved with a series
of very lively amorous scenes. With each draught that the
young lady swallowed these engravings became increasingly
visible, and the Court looked on with interest, every time she
put her nose in the cup, to see whether she blushed at what
the ebbing wine revealed. If the debutante blushed, they
laughed at her for her innocence; if she did not, she was
laughed at for being too knowing.'

'Do you propose,' asked Anne, 'that the custom should
be revived at Buckingham Palace?'

'I do not,' said Mr Scogan. 'I merely quoted the anecdote
as an illustration of the customs, so genially frank, of the
sixteenth century. I might have quoted other anecdotes to
show that the customs of the seventeenth and eighteenth, of
the fifteenth and fourteenth centuries, and indeed of every
other century, from the time of Hammurabi onward, were
equally genial and equally frank. The only century in which
customs were not characterized by the same cheerful openness was the nineteenth, of blessed memory. It was the
astonishing exception. And yet, with what one must suppose
was a deliberate disregard of history, it looked upon its horribly pregnant silences as normal and natural and right; the
frankness of the previous fifteen or twenty thousand years
was considered abnormal and perverse. It was a curious
phenomenon.'

'I entirely agree.' Mary panted with excitement in her
effort to bring out what she had to say. 'Havelock Ellis
says . . .'

Mr Scogan, like a policeman arresting the flow of traffic,
held up his hand. 'He does; I know. And that brings me to
my next point : the nature of the reaction.'

'Havelock Ellis . . .'

'The reaction, when it came – and we may say roughly that it set in a little before the beginning of this century – the reaction was to openness, but not to the same openness as had reigned in the earlier ages. It was to a scientific openness, not to the jovial frankness of the past, that we returned. The whole question of Amour became a terribly serious one. Earnest young men wrote in the public prints that from this time forth it would be impossible ever again to make a joke of any sexual matter. Professors wrote thick books in which sex was sterilized and dissected. It has become customary for serious young women, like Mary, to discuss, with philosophic calm, matters of which the merest hint would have sufficed to throw the youth of the sixties into a delirium of amorous excitement. It is all very estimable, no doubt. But still' – Mr Scogan sighed – 'I for one should like to see, mingled with this scientific ardour, a little more of the jovial spirit of Rabelais and Chaucer.'

'I entirely disagree with you,' said Mary. 'Sex isn't a laughing matter; it's serious.'

'Perhaps,' answered Mr Scogan, 'perhaps I'm an obscene old man, for I must confess that I cannot always regard it as wholly serious.'

'But I tell you . . .' began Mary furiously. Her face had flushed with excitement. Her cheeks were the cheeks of a great ripe peach.

'Indeed,' Mr Scogan continued, 'it seems to me one of the few permanently and everlasting amusing subjects that exist. Amour is the one human activity of any importance in which laughter and pleasure preponderate, if ever so slightly, over misery and pain.'

'I entirely disagree,' said Mary. There was a silence.

Anne looked at her watch. 'Nearly a quarter to eight,' she said. 'I wonder when Ivor will turn up.' She got up from her deck-chair and, leaning her elbows on the balustrade of the terrace, looked out over the valley and towards the farther hills. Under the level evening light the architecture of the land revealed itself. The deep shadows, the bright contrasting lights gave the hills a new solidity. Irregularities of the surface, unsuspected before, were picked out with light and shade. The grass, the corn, the foliage of trees were stippled with intricate shadows. The surface of things had taken on a marvellous enrichment.

'Look!' said Anne suddenly, and pointed. On the opposite side of the valley, at the crest of the ridge, a cloud of dust flushed by the sunlight to rosy gold was moving rapidly along the sky-line. 'It's Ivor. One can tell by the speed.'

The dust cloud descended into the valley and was lost. A horn with the voice of a sea-lion made itself heard, approaching. A minute later Ivor came leaping round the corner of the house. His hair waved in the wind of his own speed; he laughed as he saw them.

'Anne darling,' he cried, and embraced her, embraced Mary, very nearly embraced Mr Scogan. 'Well, here I am. I've come with incredulous speed.' Ivor's vocabulary was rich, but a little erratic. 'I'm not late for dinner, am I?' He hoisted himself up on to the balustrade, and sat there, kicking his heels. With one arm he embraced a large stone flowerpot, leaning his head sideways against its hard and lichenous flanks in an attitude of trustful affection. He had brown, wavy hair, and his eyes were of a very brilliant, pale, improbable blue. His head was narrow, his face thin and rather long, his nose aquiline. In old age – though it was difficult to imagine Ivor old – he might grow to have an Iron Ducal grimness. But now, at twenty-six, it was not the structure of his face that impressed one; it was its expression. That was charming and vivacious, and his smile was an irradiation. He was for ever moving, restlessly and rapidly, but with an engaging gracefulness. His frail and slender body seemed to be fed by a spring of inexhaustible energy.

'No, you're not late.'

'You're in time to answer a question,' said Mr Scogan. 'We were arguing whether Amour were a serious matter or no. What do you think? Is it serious?'

'Serious?' echoed Ivor. 'Most certainly.'

'I told you so,' cried Mary triumphantly.

'But in what sense serious?' Mr Scogan asked.

'I mean as an occupation. One can go on with it without ever getting bored.'

'I see,' said Mr Scogan. 'Perfectly.'

'One can occupy oneself with it,' Ivor continued, 'always and everywhere. Women are always wonderfully the same.

Shapes vary a little, that's all. In Spain' – with his free hand he described a series of ample curves – 'one can't pass them on the stairs. In England' – he put the tip of his forefinger against the tip of his thumb and, lowering his hand, drew out this circle into an imaginary cylinder – 'in England they're tubular. But their sentiments are always the same. At least, I've always found it so.'

'I'm delighted to hear it,' said Mr Scogan.

CHAPTER XVI

The ladies had left the room and the port was circulating. Mr Scogan filled his glass, passed on the decanter, and, leaning back in his chair, looked about him for a moment in silence. The conversation rippled idly round him, but he disregarded it; he was smiling at some private joke. Gombauld noticed his smile.

'What's amusing you?' he asked.

'I was just looking at you all, sitting round this table,' said Mr Scogan.

'Are we as comic as all that?'

'Not at all,' Mr Scogan answered politely. 'I was merely amused by my own speculations.'

'And what were they?'

'The idlest, the most academic of speculations. I was looking at you one by one and trying to imagine which of the first Caesars you would each resemble, if you were given the opportunity of behaving like a Caesar. The Caesars are one of my touchstones,' Mr Scogan explained. 'They are characters functioning, so to speak, in the void. They are human beings developed to their logical conclusions. Hence their unequalled value as a touchstone, a standard. When I meet someone for the first time, I ask myself this question : Given the Caesarean environment, which of the Caesars would this person resemble – Julius, Augustus, Tiberius, Caligula, Claudius, Nero? I take each trait of character, each mental and emotional bias, each little oddity, and magnify them a thousand times. The resulting image gives me his Caesarean formula.'

'And which of the Caesars do you resemble?' asked Gombauld.

'I am potentially all of them,' Mr Scogan replied, 'all – with the possible exception of Claudius, who was much too stupid to be a development of anything in my character. The seeds of Julius's courage and compelling energy, of Augustus's prudence, of the libidinousness and cruelty of Tiberius, of Caligula's folly, of Nero's artistic genius and enormous vanity, are all within me. Given the opportunities, I might have been something fabulous. But circumstances were against me. I was born and brought up in a country rectory; I passed my youth doing a great deal of utterly senseless hard work for a very little money. The result is that now, in middle age, I am the poor thing that I am. But perhaps it is as well. Perhaps, too, it's as well that Denis hasn't been permitted to flower into a little Nero, and that Ivor remains only potentially a Caligula. Yes, it's better so, no doubt. But it would have been more amusing, as a spectacle, if they had had the chance to develop, untrammelled, the full horror of their potentialities. It would have been pleasant and interesting to watch their tics and foibles and little vices swelling and burgeoning and blossoming into enormous and fantastic flowers of cruelty and pride and lewdness and avarice. The Caesaraean environment makes the Caesar, as the special food and the queenly cell make the queen bee. We differ from the bees in so far that, given the proper food, they can be sure of making a queen every time. With us there is no such certainty; out of every ten men placed in the Caesarean environment one will be temperamentally good, or intelligent, or great. The rest will blossom into Caesars; he will not. Seventy and eighty years ago simple-minded people, reading of the exploits of the Bourbons in South Italy, cried out in amazement: To think that such things should be happening in the nineteenth century! And a few years since we too were astonished to find that in our still more astonishing twentieth century, unhappy blackamoors on the Congo and the Amazon were being treated as English serfs were treated in the time of Stephen. Today we are no longer surprised at these things. The Black and Tans harry Ireland, the Poles maltreat the Silesians, the bold Fascisti slaughter their poorer countrymen: we take it all for granted. Since the war we wonder at nothing. We have created a Caesarean environment and a host of little Caesars has sprung up. What could be more natural?'

Mr Scogan drank off what was left of his port and refilled the glass.

'At this very moment,' he went on, 'the most frightful horrors are taking place in every corner of the world. People are being crushed, slashed, disembowelled, mangled; their dead bodies rot and their eyes decay with the rest. Screams of pain and fear go pulsing through the air at the rate of eleven hundred feet per second. After travelling for three seconds they are perfectly inaudible. These are distressing facts; but do we enjoy life any the less because of them? Most certainly we do not. We feel sympathy, no doubt; we represent to ourselves imaginatively the sufferings of nations and individuals and we deplore them. But, after all, what are sympathy and imagination? Precious little, unless the person for whom we feel sympathy happens to be closely involved in our affections; and even then they don't go very far. And a good thing too; for if one had an imagination vivid enough and a sympathy sufficiently sensitive really to comprehend and to feel the sufferings of other people, one would never have a moment's peace of mind. A really sympathetic race would not so much as know the meaning of happiness. But luckily, as I've already said, we aren't a sympathetic race. At the beginning of the war I used to think I really suffered, through imagination and sympathy, with those who physically suffered. But after a month or two I had to admit that, honestly, I didn't. And yet I think I have a more vivid imagination than most. One is always alone in suffering; the fact is depressing when one happens to be the sufferer, but it makes pleasure possible for the rest of the world.'

There was a pause. Henry Wimbush pushed back his chair.

'I think perhaps we ought to go and join the ladies,' he said.

'So do I,' said Ivor, jumping up with alacrity. He turned to Mr Scogan. 'Fortunately,' he said, 'we can share our pleasures. We are not always condemned to be happy alone.'

CHAPTER XVII

Ivor brought his hands down with a bang on to the final chord of his rhapsody. There was just a hint in that triumphant harmony that the seventh had been struck along with the octave by the thumb of the left hand; but the general effect of splendid noise emerged clearly enough. Small details matter little so long as the general effect is good. And, besides, that hint of the seventh was decidedly modern. He turned round in his seat and tossed the hair back out of his eyes.

'There,' he said. 'That's the best I can do for you, I'm afraid.'

Murmurs of applause and gratitude were heard, and Mary, her large china eyes fixed on the performer, cried out aloud, 'Wonderful!' and gasped for new breath as though she were suffocating.

Nature and fortune had vied with one another in heaping on Ivor Lombard all their choicest gifts. He had wealth and he was perfectly independent. He was good looking, possessed an irresistible charm of manner, and was the hero of more amorous successes than he could well remember. His accomplishments were extraordinary for their number and variety. He had a beautiful untrained tenor voice; he could improvise, with a startling brilliance, rapidly and loudly, on the piano. He was a good amateur medium and telepathist, and had a considerable first-hand knowledge of the next world. He could write rhymed verses with an extraordinary rapidity. For painting symbolical pictures he had a dashing style, and if the drawing was sometimes a little weak, the colour was always pyrotechnical. He excelled in amateur theatricals and, when occasion offered, he could cook with genius. He resembled Shakespeare in knowing little Latin and less Greek. For a mind like his, education seemed supererogatory. Training would only have destroyed his natural aptitudes.

'Let's go out into the garden,' Ivor suggested. 'It's a wonderful night.'

'Thank you,' said Mr Scogan, 'but I for one prefer these

still more wonderful arm-chairs.' His pipe had begun to bubble oozily every time he pulled at it. He was perfectly happy.

Henry Wimbush was also happy. He looked for a moment over his pince-nez in Ivor's direction and then, without saying anything, returned to the grimy little sixteenth-century account books which were now his favourite reading. He knew more about Sir Ferdinando's household expenses than about his own.

The outdoor party, enrolled under Ivor's banner, consisted of Anne, Mary, Denis, and, rather unexpectedly, Jenny. Outside it was warm and dark; there was no moon. They walked up and down the terrace, and Ivor sang a Neapolitan song : 'Stretti, stretti' – close, close – with something about the little Spanish girl to follow. The atmosphere began to palpitate. Ivor put his arm round Anne's waist, dropped his head sideways on to her shoulder, and in that position walked on, singing as he walked. It seemed the easiest, the most natural, thing in the world. Denis wondered why he had never done it. He hated Ivor.

'Let's go down to the pool,' said Ivor. He disengaged his embrace and turned round to shepherd his little flock. They made their way along the side of the house to the entrance of the yew-tree walk that led down to the lower garden. Between the blank precipitous wall of the house and the tall yew trees the path was a chasm of impenetrable gloom. Somewhere there were steps down to the right, a gap in the yew hedge. Denis, who headed the party, groped his way cautiously; in this darkness, one had an irrational fear of yawning precipices, of horrible spiked obstructions. Suddenly from behind him he heard a shrill, startled, 'Oh !' and then a sharp, dry concussion that might have been the sound of a slap. After that, Jenny's voice was heard pronouncing, 'I am going back to the house.' Her tone was decided, and even as she pronounced the words she was melting away into the darkness. The incident, whatever it had been, was closed. Denis resumed his forward groping. From somewhere behind Ivor began to sing again, softly :

> 'Phillis plus avare que tendre,
> Ne gagnant rien à refuser,

Un jour exigea à Silvandre
Trente moutons pour un baiser.'

The melody drooped and climbed again with a kind of easy languor; the warm darkness seemed to pulse like blood about them.

'Le lendemain, nouvelle affaire :
Pour le berger, le troc fut bon . . ;'

'Here are the steps,' cried Denis. He guided his companions over the danger, and in a moment they had the turf of the yew-tree walk under their feet. It was lighter here, or at least it was just perceptibly less dark; for the yew walk was wider than the path that had led them under the lea of the house. Looking up, they could see between the high black hedges a strip of sky and a few stars.

'Car il obtint de la bergère . . .'

went on Ivor, and then interrupted himself to shout, 'I'm going to run down,' and he was off, full speed, down the invisible slope, singing unevenly as he went :

'Trente baisers pour un mouton.'

The others followed. Denis shambled in the rear, vainly exhorting everyone to caution : the slope was steep, one might break one's neck. What was wrong with these people, he wondered? They had become like young kittens after a dose of cat-nip. He himself felt a certain kittenishness sporting within him; but it was, like all his emotions, rather a theoretical feeling; it did not overmasteringly seek to express itself in a practical demonstration of kittenishness.

'Be careful,' he shouted once more, and hardly were the words out of his mouth when, thump ! there was the sound of a heavy fall in front of him, followed by the long 'F-f-f-f-f' of a breath indrawn with pain and afterwards by a very sincere, 'Oo-ooh !' Denis was almost pleased ; he had told them so, the idiots, and they wouldn't listen. He trotted down the slope towards the unseen sufferer.

Mary came down the hill like a runaway steam-engine. It was tremendously exciting, this blind rush through the dark;

91

she felt she would never stop. But the ground grew level beneath her feet, her speed insensibly slackened, and suddenly she was caught by an extended arm and brought to an abrupt halt.

'Well,' said Ivor as he tightened his embrace, 'you're caught now, Anne.'

She made an effort to release herself. 'It's not Anne. It's Mary.'

Ivor burst into a peal of amused laughter. 'So it is !' he exclaimed. 'I seem to be making nothing but floaters this evening. I've already made one with Jenny.' He laughed again, and there was something so jolly about his laughter that Mary could not help laughing too. He did not remove his encircling arm, and somehow it was all so amusing and natural that Mary made no further attempt to escape from it. They walked along by the side of the pool, interlaced. Mary was too short for him to be able, with any comfort, to lay his head on her shoulder. He rubbed his cheek, caressed and caressing, against the thick, sleek mass of her hair. In a little while he began to sing again; the night trembled amorously to the sound of his voice. When he had finished he kissed her. Anne or Mary : Mary or Anne. It didn't seem to make much difference which it was. There were differences in detail, of course; but the general effect was the same; and, after all, the general effect was the important thing.

Denis made his way down the hill.

'Any damage done?' he called out.

'Is that you, Denis? I've hurt my ankle so – and my knee, and my hand. I'm all in pieces.'

'My poor Anne,' he said. 'But then,' he couldn't help adding, 'it was silly to start running downhill in the dark.'

'Ass !' she retorted in a tone of tearful irritation; 'of course it was.'

He sat down beside her on the grass, and found himself breathing the faint, delicious atmosphere of perfume that she carried always with her.

'Light a match,' she commanded. 'I want to look at my wounds.'

He felt in his pockets for the match-box. The light spurted and then grew steady. Magically, a little universe had been created, a world of colours and forms – Anne's face, the shimmering orange of her dress, her white, bare arms, a patch of green turf – and round about a darkness that had become solid and utterly blind. Anne held out her hands; both were green and earthy with her fall, and the left exhibited two or three red abrasions.

'Not so bad,' she said. But Denis was terribly distressed, and his emotion was intensified when, looking up at her face, he saw that the trace of tears, involuntary tears of pain, lingered on her eyelashes. He pulled out his handkerchief and began to wipe away the dirt from the wounded hand. The match went out; it was not worth while to light another. Anne allowed herself to be attended to, meekly and gratefully. 'Thank you,' she said, when he had finished cleaning and bandaging her hand; and there was something in her tone that made him feel that she had lost her superiority over him, that she was younger than he, had become, suddenly, almost a child. He felt tremendously large and protective. The feeling was so strong that instinctively he put his arm about her. She drew closer, leaned against him, and so they sat in silence. Then, from below, soft but wonderfully clear through the still darkness, they heard the sound of Ivor's singing. He was going on with his half-finished song :

> 'Le lendemain Phillis plus tendre,
> Ne voulant déplaire au berger,
> Fut trop heureuse de lui rendre
> Trente moutons pour un baiser.'

There was a rather prolonged pause. It was as though time were being allowed for the giving and receiving of a few of those thirty kisses. Then the voice sang on :

> 'Le lendemain Phillis peu sage
> Aurait donné moutons et chien
> Pour un baiser que le volage
> A Lisette donnait pour rien.'

The last note died away into an uninterrupted silence.

'Are you better?' Denis whispered. 'Are you comfortable like this?'

She nodded a Yes to both questions.

'Trente moutons pour un baiser.' The sheep, the woolly mutton – baa, baa, baa . . . ? Or the shepherd? Yes, decidedly, he felt himself to be the shepherd now. He was the master, the protector. A wave of courage swelled through him, warm as wine. He turned his head, and began to kiss her face, at first rather randomly, then, with more precision, on the mouth.

Anne averted her head; he kissed the ear, the smooth nape that this movement presented him. 'No,' she protested; 'no, Denis.'

'Why not?'

'It spoils our friendship, and that was so jolly.'

'Bosh!' said Denis.

She tried to explain. 'Can't you see,' she said, 'it isn't . . . it isn't our stunt at all.' It was true. Somehow she had never thought of Denis in the light of a man who might make love; she had never so much as conceived the possibilities of an amorous relationship with him. He was so absurdly young, so . . . so . . . she couldn't find the adjective, but she knew what she meant.

'Why isn't it our stunt?' asked Denis. 'And, by the way, that's a horrible and inappropriate expression.'

'Because it isn't.'

'But if I say it is?'

'It makes no difference. I say it isn't.'

'I shall make you say it is.'

'All right, Denis. But you must do it another time. I must go in and get my ankle into hot water. It's beginning to swell.'

Reasons of health could not be gainsaid. Denis got up reluctantly, and helped his companion to her feet. She took a cautious step. 'Ooh!' She halted and leaned heavily on his arm.

'I'll carry you,' Denis offered. He had never tried to carry a woman, but on the cinema it always looked an easy piece of heroism.

'You couldn't,' said Anne.

'Of course I can.' He felt larger and more protective than ever. 'Put your arms round my neck,' he ordered. She did so and, stooping, he picked her up under the knees and lifted her from the ground. Good heavens, what a weight! He took

five staggering steps up the slope, then almost lost his equili-
brium, and had to deposit his burden suddenly, with something of a bump.

Anne was shaking with laughter. 'I said you couldn't,
my poor Denis.'

'I can,' said Denis, without conviction. 'I'll try again.'

'It's perfectly sweet of you to offer, but I'd rather walk,
thanks.' She laid her hand on his shoulder and, thus supported, began to limp slowly up the hill.

'My poor Denis!' she repeated, and laughed again.
Humili ted, he was silent. It seemed incredible that, only
two minutes ago, he should have been holding her in his embrace, kissing her. Incredible. She was helpless then, a child.
Now she had regained all her superiority; she was once more
the far-off being, desired and unassailable. Why had he been
such a fool as to suggest that carrying stunt? He reached the
house in a state of the profoundest depression.

He helped Anne upstairs, left her in the hands of a maid,
and came down again to the drawing-room. He was surprised to find them all sitting just where he had left them.
He had expected that, somehow, everything would be quite
different – it seemed such a prodigious time since he went
away. All silent and all damned, he reflected, as he looked at
them. Mr Scogan's pipe still wheezed; that was the only
sound. Henry Wimbush was still deep in his account books;
he had just made the discovery that Sir Ferdinando was in
the habit of eating oysters the whole summer through, re-
gardless of the absence of the justifying R. Gombauld, in
horn-rimmed spectacles, was reading. Jenny was mysteriously
scribbling in her red notebook. And, seated in her favourite
arm-chair at the corner of the hearth, Priscilla was looking
through a pile of drawings. One by one she held them out
at arm's length and, throwing back her mountainous orange
head, looked long and attentively through half-closed eyelids. She wore a pale sea-green dress; on the slope of her
mauve-powdered décolletage diamonds twinkled. An immensely long cigarette-holder projected at an angle from her
face. Diamonds were embedded in her high-piled coiffure;
they glittered every time she moved. It was a batch of Ivor's
drawings – sketches of Spirit Life, made in the course of
tranced tours through the other world. On the back of each

sheet descriptive titles were written : 'Portrait of an Angel, 15th March '20'; 'Astral Beings at Play, 3rd December '19'; 'A Party of Souls on their Way to a Higher Sphere, 21st May '21.' Before examining the drawing on the obverse of each sheet, she turned it over to read the title. Try as she could – and she tried hard – Priscilla had never seen a vision or succeeded in establishing any communication with the Spirit World. She had to be content with the reported experiences of others.

'What have you done with the rest of your party?' she asked, looking up as Denis entered the room.

He explained. Anne had gone to bed, Ivor and Mary were still in the garden. He selected a book and a comfortable chair, and tried, as far as the disturbed state of his mind would permit him, to compose himself for an evening's reading. The lamplight was utterly serene; there was no movement save the stir of Priscilla among her papers. All silent and all damned, Denis repeated to himself, all silent and all damned. . . .

It was nearly an hour later when Ivor and Mary made their appearance.

'We waited to see the moon rise,' said Ivor.

'It was gibbous, you know,' Mary explained, very technical and scientific.

'It was so beautiful down in the garden ! The trees, the scent of the flowers, the stars . . .' Ivor waved his arms. 'And when the moon came up, it was really too much. It made me burst into tears.' He sat down at the piano and opened the lid.

'There were a great many meteorites,' said Mary to anyone who would listen. 'The earth must just be coming into the summer shower of them. In July and August . . .'

But Ivor had already begun to strike the keys. He played the garden, the stars, the scent of flowers, the rising moon. He even put in a nightingale that was not there. Mary looked on and listened with parted lips. The others pursued their occupations, without appearing to be seriously disturbed. On this very July day, exactly three hundred and fifty years ago, Sir Ferdinando had eaten seven dozen oysters. The discovery of this fact gave Henry Wimbush a peculiar pleasure. He had a natural piety which made him delight in the celebration of memorial feasts. The three hundred and fiftieth anniversay of the seven dozen oysters. . . . He wished he had known before dinner; he would have ordered champagne.

On her way to bed Mary paid a call. The light was out in Anne's room, but she was not yet asleep.

'Why didn't you come down to the garden with us?' Mary asked.

'I fell down and twisted my ankle. Denis helped me home.'

Mary was full of sympathy. Inwardly, too, she was relieved to find Anne's non-appearance so simply accounted for. She had been vaguely suspicious, down there in the garden – suspicious of what, she hardly knew; but there had seemed to be something a little *louche* in the way she had suddenly found herself alone with Ivor. Not that she minded, of course; far from it. But she didn't like the idea that perhaps she was the victim of a put-up job.

'I do hope you'll be better tomorrow,' she said, and she commiserated with Anne on all she had missed – the garden, the stars, the scent of flowers, the meteorites through whose summer shower the earth was now passing, the rising moon and its gibbosity. And then they had had such interesting conversation. What about? About almost everything. Nature, art, science, poetry, the stars, spiritualism, the relations of the sexes, music, religion. Ivor, she thought, had an interesting mind.

The two young ladies parted affectionately.

CHAPTER XVIII

The nearest Roman Catholic church was upwards of twenty miles away. Ivor, who was punctilious in his devotions, came down early to breakfast and had his car at the door, ready to start, by a quarter to ten. It was a smart, expensive-looking machine, enamelled a pure lemon yellow and upholstered in emerald green leather. There were two seats – three if you squeezed tightly enough – and their occupants were protected from wind, dust, and weather by a glazed sedan that rose, an elegant eighteenth-century hump, from the midst of the body of the car.

Mary had never been to a Roman Catholic service, thought it would be an interesting experience, and, when the car moved off through the great gates of the courtyard, she was occupying the spare seat in the sedan. The sea-lion horn roared, faintlier, faintlier, and they were gone.

In the parish church of Crome Mr Bodiham preached on 1 Kings vi. 18 : 'And the cedar of the house within was carved with knops' – a sermon of immediate local interest. For the past two years the problem of the War Memorial had exercised the minds of all those in Crome who had enough leisure, or mental energy, or party spirit to think of such things. Henry Wimbush was all for a library – a library of local literature, stocked with county histories, old maps of the district, monographs on the local antiquities, dialect dictionaries, handbooks of the local geology and natural history. He liked to think of the villagers, inspired by such reading, making up parties of a Sunday afternoon to look for fossils and flint arrow-heads. The villagers themselves favoured the idea of a memorial reservoir and water supply. But the busiest and most articulate party followed Mr Bodiham in demanding something religious in character – a second lich-gate, for example, a stained-glass window, a monument of marble, or, if possible, all three. So far, however, nothing had been done, partly because the memorial committee had never been able to agree, partly for the more cogent reason that too little money had been subscribed to carry out any of the proposed schemes. Every three or four months Mr Bodiham preached a sermon on the subject. His last had been delivered in March; it was high time that his congregation had a fresh reminder.

'And the cedar of the house within was carved with knops.' Mr Bodiham touched lightly on Solomon's temple. From thence he passed to temples and churches in general. What were the characteristics of these buildings dedicated to God? Obviously, the fact of their, from a human point of view, complete uselessness. They were unpractical buildings 'carved with knops.' Solomon might have built a library – indeed, what could be more to the taste of the world's wisest man? He might have dug a reservoir – what more useful in a parched city like Jerusalem? He did neither; he built a house all carved with knops, useless and unpractical. Why? Because he was dedicating the work to God. There had been much talk in Crome about the proposed War Memorial. A War Memorial was, in its very nature, a work dedicated to God. It was a token of thankfulness that the first stage in the culminating world-war had been crowned by the triumph of righteousness; it was at the same time a visibly embodied supplication that God might not long delay the Advent which alone could bring the final peace. A library, a reservoir? Mr Bodiham scornfully and indignantly condemned the idea. These were works dedicated to man, not to God. As a War Memorial they were totally unsuitable. A lich-gate had been suggested. This was an object which answered perfectly to the definition of a War Memorial : a useless work dedicated to God and carved with knops. One lich-gate, it was true, already existed. But nothing would be easier than to make a second entrance into the churchyard; and a second entrance would need a second gate. Other suggestions had been made. Stained-glass windows, a monument of marble. Both these were admirable, especially the latter. It was high time that the War Memorial was erected. It might soon be too late. At any moment, like a thief in the night, God might come. Meanwhile a difficulty stood in the way. Funds were inadequate. All should subscribe according to their means. Those who had lost relations in the war might reasonably be expected to subscribe a sum equal to that which they would have had to pay in funeral expenses if

99

the relative had died while at home. Further delay was disastrous. The War Memorial must be built at once. He appealed to the patriotism and the Christian sentiments of all his hearers.

Henry Wimbush walked home thinking of the books he would present to the War Memorial Library, if ever it came into existence. He took the path through the fields; it was pleasanter than the road. At the first stile a group of village boys, loutish young fellows all dressed in the hideous ill-fitting black which makes a funeral of every English Sunday and holiday, were assembled, drearily guffawing as they smoked their cigarettes. They made way for Henry Wimbush, touching their caps as he passed. He returned their salute; his bowler and face were one in their unruffled gravity.

In Sir Ferdinando's time, he reflected, in the time of his son, Sir Julius, these young men would have had their Sunday diversions even at Crome, remote and rustic Crome. There would have been archery, skittles, dancing – social amusements in which they would have partaken as members of a conscious community. Now they had nothing, nothing except Mr Bodiham's forbidding Boys' Club and the rare dances and concerts organized by himself. Boredom or the urban pleasures of the county metropolis were the alternatives that presented themselves to these poor youths. Country pleasures were no more; they had been stamped out by the Puritans.

In Manningham's Diary for 1600 there was a queer passage, he remembered, a very queer passage. Certain magistrates in Berkshire, Puritan magistrates, had had wind of a scandal. One moonlit summer night they had ridden out with their *posse* and there, among the hills, they had come upon a company of men and women, dancing, stark naked, among the sheep-cotes. The magistrates and their men had ridden their horses into the crowd. How self-conscious the poor people must suddenly have felt, how helpless without their clothes against armed and booted horsemen! The dancers are arrested, whipped, gaoled, set in the stocks; the moonlight dance is never danced again. What old, earthy, Panic rite came to extinction here? he wondered. Who knows? – perhaps their ancestors had danced like this in the moonlight ages before Adam and Eve were so much as thought of. He liked to think so. And now it was no more. These weary young men, if they wanted to dance, would have to bicycle six miles to the town. The country was desolate, without life of its own, without indigenous pleasures. The pious magistrates had snuffed out for ever a little happy flame that had burned from the beginning of time.

> 'And as on Tullia's tomb one lamp burned clear,
>   Unchanged for fifteen hundred year . . .'

He repeated the lines to himself, and was desolated to think of all the murdered past.

CHAPTER XIX

Henry Wimbush's long cigar burned aromatically. The *History of Crome* lay on his knee; slowly be turned over the pages.

'I can't decide what episode to read you tonight,' he said thoughtfully. 'Sir Ferdinando's voyages are not without interest. Then, of course, there's his son, Sir Julius. It was he who suffered from the delusion that his perspiration engendered flies; it drove him finally to suicide. Or there's Sir Cyprian.' He turned the pages more rapidly. 'Or Sir Henry. Or Sir George. . . . No, I'm inclined to think I won't read about any of these.'

'But you must read something,' insisted Mr Scogan, taking his pipe out of his mouth.

'I think I shall read about my grandfather,' said Henry Wimbush, 'and the events that led up to his marriage with the eldest daughter of the last Sir Ferdinando.'

'Good,' said Mr Scogan. 'We are listening.'

'Before I begin reading,' said Henry Wimbush, looking up from the book and taking off the pince-nez which he had just fitted to his nose — 'before I begin, I must say a few preliminary words about Sir Ferdinando, the last of the Lapiths. At the death of the virtuous and unfortunate Sir Hercules, Ferdinando found himself in possession of the family fortune, not a little increased by his father's temperance and thrift; he applied himself forthwith to the task of spending it, which he did in an ample and jovial fashion. By the time he was forty he had eaten and, above all, drunk and loved away about half his capital, and would infallibly have soon got rid of the rest in the same manner, if he had not had the good fortune to become so madly enamoured of the Rector's daughter as to make a proposal of marriage. The young lady accepted him, and in less than a year had become the absolute mistress of Crome and her husband. An extraordinary reformation made itself apparent in Sir Ferdinando's character. He grew regular and economical in his habits; he even became temperate, rarely drinking more than a

bottle and a half of port at a sitting. The waning fortune of
the Lapiths began once more to wax, and that in despite of
the hard times (for Sir Ferdinando married in 1809 in the
height of the Napoleonic Wars). A prosperous and dignified
old age, cheered by the spectacle of his children's growth and
happiness – for Lady Lapith had already borne him three
daughters, and there seemed no good reason why she should
not bear many more of them, and sons as well – a patriarchal
decline into the family vault, seemed now to be Sir Ferdinando's enviable destiny. But Providence willed otherwise.
To Napoleon, cause already of such infinite mischief, was
due, though perhaps indirectly, the untimely and violent
death which put a period to this reformed existence.

'Sir Ferdinando, who was above all things a patriot, had
adopted, from the earliest days of the conflict with the
French, his own peculiar method of celebrating our victories.
When the happy news reached London, it was his custom
to purchase immediately a large store of liquor and, taking a
place on whichever of the outgoing coaches he happened to
light on first, to drive through the country proclaiming the
good news to all he met on the road and dispensing it, along
with the liquor, at every stopping-place to all who cared to
listen or drink. Thus, after the Nile, he had driven as far as
Edinburgh; and later, when the coaches, wreathed with
laurel for triumph, with cypress for mourning, were setting
out with the news of Nelson's victory and death, he sat
through all a chilly October night in the box of the Norwich
Meteor with a nautical keg of rum on his knees and two
cases of old brandy under the seat. This genial custom was
one of the many habits which he abandoned on his marriage.
The victories in the Peninsula, the retreat from Moscow,
Leipzig, and the abdication of the tyrant all went uncele-
brated. It so happened, however, that in the summer of 1815
Sir Ferdinando was staying for a few weeks in the capital.
There had been a succession of anxious, doubtful days; then
came the glorious news of Waterloo. It was too much for
Sir Ferdinando; his joyous youth awoke again within him.
He hurried to his wine merchant and bought a dozen bottles
of 1760 brandy. The Bath coach was on the point of start-
ing; he bribed his way on to the box and, seated in glory
beside the driver, proclaimed aloud the downfall of the

Corsican bandit and passed about the warm liquid joy. They clattered through Uxbridge, Slough, Maidenhead. Sleeping Reading was awakened by the great news. At Didcot one of the ostlers was so much overcome by patriotic emotions and the 1760 brandy that he found it impossible to do up the buckles of the harness. The night began to grow chilly, and Sir Ferdinando found that it was not enough to take a nip at every stage : to keep up his vital warmth he was compelled to drink between the stages as well. They were approaching Swindon. The coach was travelling at a dizzy speed – six miles in the last half-hour – when, without having manifested the slightest premonitory symptom of unsteadiness, Sir Ferdinando suddenly toppled sideways off his seat and fell, head foremost, into the road. An unpleasant jolt awakened the slumbering passengers. The coach was brought to a standstill; the guard ran back with a light. He found Sir Ferdinando still alive, but unconscious; blood was oozing from his mouth. The back wheels of the coach had passed over his body, breaking most of his ribs and both arms. His skull was fractured in two places. They picked him up, but he was dead before they reached the next stage. So perished Sir Ferdinando, a victim to his own patriotism. Lady Lapith did not marry again, but determined to devote the rest of her life to the well-being of her three children – Georgiana, now five years old, and Emmeline and Caroline, twins of two.'

Henry Wimbush paused, and once more put on his pince-nez. 'So much by way of introduction,' he said. 'Now I can begin to read about my grandfather.'

'One moment,' said Mr Scogan, 'till I've refilled my pipe.'

Mr Wimbush waited. Seated apart in a corner of the room, Ivor was showing Mary his sketches of Spirit Life. They spoke together in whispers.

Mr Scogan had lighted his pipe again. 'Fire away,' he said.

Henry Wimbush fired away.

'It was in the spring of 1833 that my grandfather, George Wimbush, first made the acquaintance of the "three lovely Lapiths," as they were always called. He was then a young man of twenty-two, with curly yellow hair and a smooth pink face that was the mirror of his youthful and ingenuous mind. He had been educated at Harrow and Christ Church, he enjoyed hunting and all other field sports, and, though his circumstances were comfortable to the verge of affluence, his pleasures were temperate and innocent. His father, an East Indian merchant, had destined him for a political career, and had gone to considerable expense in acquiring a pleasant little Cornish borough as a twenty-first birthday gift for his son. He was justly indignant when, on the very eve of George's majority, the Reform Bill of 1832 swept the borough out of existence. The inauguration of George's political career had to be postponed. At the time he got to know the lovely Lapiths he was waiting; he was not at all impatient.

'The lovely Lapiths did not fail to impress him. Georgiana, the eldest, with her black ringlets, her flashing eyes, her noble aquiline profile, her swan-like neck, and sloping shoulders, was orientally dazzling; and the twins, with their delicately turned-up noses, their blue eyes, and chestnut hair, were an identical pair of ravishingly English charmers.

'Their conversation at this first meeting proved, however, to be so forbidding that, but for the invincible attraction exercised by their beauty, George would never have had the courage to follow up the acquaintance. The twins, looking up their noses at him with an air of languid superiority, asked him what he thought of the latest French poetry and whether he liked the *Indiana* of George Sand. But what was almost worse was the question with which Georgiana opened her conversation with him. "In music," she asked, leaning forward and fixing him with her large dark eyes, "are you a classicist or a transcendentalist?" George did not lose his presence of mind. He had enough appreciation of music to know that he hated anything classical, and so, with a promptitude which did him credit, he replied, "I am a transcendentalist." Georgiana smiled bewitchingly. "I am glad," she said; "so am I. You went to hear Paganini last week, of course. 'The Prayer of Moses' – ah!" She closed her eyes. "Do you know anything more transcendental than that?" "No," said George, "I don't." He hesitated, was about to go on speaking, and then decided that after all it would be wiser not to say – what was in fact true – that he had enjoyed above all Paganini's Farmyard Imitations. The man had made his fiddle bray like an ass, cluck like a hen, grunt, squeal, bark, neigh, quack, bellow, and growl; that last item, in George's estimation, had almost compensated for the tediousness of the rest of the concert. He smiled with pleasure at the thought of it. Yes, decidedly, he was no classicist in music; he was a thoroughgoing transcendentalist.

'George followed up this first introduction by paying a call on the young ladies and their mother, who occupied, during the season, a small but elegant house in the neighbourhood of Berkeley Square. Lady Lapith made a few discreet inquiries, and having found that George's financial position, character, and family were all passably good, she asked him to dine. She hoped and expected that her daughters would all marry into the peerage; but, being a prudent woman, she knew it was advisable to prepare for all contingencies. George Wimbush, she thought, would make an excellent second string for one of the twins.

'At this first dinner, George's partner was Emmeline. They talked of Nature. Emmeline protested that to her high mountains were a feeling and the hum of human cities torture. George agreed that the country was very agreeable, but held that London during the season also had its charms. He noticed with surprise and a certain solicitous distress that Miss Emmeline's appetite was poor, that it didn't, in fact, exist. Two spoonfuls of soup, a morsel of fish, no bird, no meat, and three grapes – that was her whole dinner. He looked from time to time at her two sisters; Georgiana and Caroline seemed to be quite as abstemious. They waved away whatever was offered them with an expression of delicate disgust, shutting their eyes and averting their faces from the proffered dish, as though the lemon sole, the duck, the loin of veal, the trifle, were objects revolting to the sight and smell. George, who thought the dinner capital, ventured to comment on the sisters' lack of appetite.

' "Pray, don't talk to me of eating," said Emmeline, drooping like a sensitive plant. "We find it so coarse, so unspiritual, my sisters and I. One can't think of one's soul while one is eating."

'George agreed; one couldn't. "But one must live," he said.

' "Alas!" Emmeline sighed. "One must. Death is very beautiful, don't you think?" She broke a corner off a piece of toast and began to nibble at it languidly. "But since, as you say, one must live . . ." She made a little gesture of resignation. "Luckily a very little suffices to keep one alive." She put down her corner of toast half eaten.

'George regarded her with some surprise. She was pale, but she looked extraordinarily healthy, he thought; so did her sisters. Perhaps if you were really spiritual you needed less food. He, clearly, was not spiritual.

'After this he saw them frequently. They all liked him, from Lady Lapith downwards. True, he was not very romantic or poetical; but he was such a pleasant, unpretentious, kind-hearted young man, that one couldn't help liking him. For his part, he thought them wonderful, wonderful, especially Georgiana. He enveloped them all in a warm, protective affection. For they needed protection; they were altogether too frail, too spiritual for this world. They never ate, they were always pale, they often complained of fever, they talked much and lovingly of death, they frequently swooned. Georgiana was the most ethereal of all; of the three she ate least, swooned most often, talked most of death, and was the palest – with a pallor that was so startling as to appear positively artificial. At any moment, it seemed, she might loose her precarious hold on this material world and become all spirit. To George the thought was a continual agony. If she were to die . . .

'She contrived, however, to live through the season, and that in spite of the numerous balls, routs, and other parties of pleasure which, in company with the rest of the lovely trio, she never failed to attend. In the middle of July the whole household moved down to the country. George was invited to spend the month of August at Crome.

'The house-party was distinguished; in the list of visitors figured the names of two marriageable young men of title. George had hoped that country air, repose, and natural surroundings might have restored to the three sisters their appetites and the roses of their cheeks. He was mistaken. For dinner, the first evening, Georgiana ate only an olive, two or three salted almonds, and half a peach. She was as pale as ever. During the meal she spoke of love.

' "True love," she said, "being infinite and eternal, can only be consummated in eternity. Indiana and Sir Rodolphe celebrated the mystic wedding of their souls by jumping into Niagara. Love is incompatible with life. The wish of two people who truly love one another is not to live together but to die together."

' "Come, come, my dear," said Lady Lapith, stout and practical. "What would become of the next generation, pray, if all the world acted on your principles?"'

' "Mamma! . . ." Georgiana protested, and dropped her eyes.

' "In my young days," Lady Lapith went on, "I should have been laughed out of countenance if I'd said a thing like that. But then in my young days souls weren't as fashionable as they are now and we didn't think death was at all poetical. It was just unpleasant."

' "Mamma! . . ." Emmeline and Caroline implored in unison.

' "In my young days—" Lady Lapith was launched into her subject; nothing, it seemed, could stop her now. "In my young days, if you didn't eat, people told you you needed a dose of rhubarb. Nowadays . . ."'

'There was a cry; Georgiana had swooned sideways on to Lord Timpany's shoulder. It was a desperate expedient; but it was successful. Lady Lapith was stopped.

'The days passed in an uneventful round of pleasures. Of all the gay party George alone was unhappy. Lord Timpany was paying his court to Georgiana, and it was clear that he was not unfavourably received. George looked on, and his soul was a hell of jealousy and despair. The boisterous company of the young men became intolerable to him; he shrank from them, seeking gloom and solitude. One morning, having broken away from them on some vague pretext, he returned to the house alone. The young men were bathing in the pool below; their cries and laughter floated up to him, making the quiet house seem lonelier and more silent. The lovely sisters and their mamma still kept their chambers; they did not customarily make their appearance till luncheon, so that the male guests had the morning to themselves. George sat down in the hall and abandoned himself to thought.

'At any moment she might die; at any moment she might become Lady Timpany. It was terrible, terrible. If she died, then he would die too; he would go to seek her beyond the grave. If she became Lady Timpany . . . ah, then! The solution of the problem would not be so simple. If she became Lady Timpany : it was a horrible thought. But then supose she were in love with Timpany – though it seemed incredible that anyone could be in love with Timpany – suppose her life depended on Timpany, suppose she couldn't live without him? He was fumbling his way along this clueless labyrinth of suppositions when the clock struck twelve. On the last stroke, like an automaton released by the turning clockwork, a little maid, holding a large covered tray, popped out of the door that led from the kitchen regions into the hall. From his deep arm-chair George watched her (himself, it was evident, unobserved) with an idle curiosity. She pattered across the room and came to a halt in front of what seemed a blank expanse of panelling. She reached out her hand and, to George's extreme astonishment, a little door swung open, revealing the foot of a winding staircase. Turning sideways in order to get her tray through the narrow opening, the little maid darted in with a rapid crablike motion. The door closed behind her with a click. A minute later it opened again and the maid, without her tray, hurried back across the hall and disappeared in the direction of the kitchen. George tried to recompose his thoughts, but an invincible curiosity drew his mind towards the hidden door, the staircase, the little maid. It was in vain he told himself that the matter was none of his business, that to explore the secrets of that surprising door, that mysterious staircase within, would be a piece of unforgivable rudeness and indiscretion. It was in vain; for five minutes he struggled heroically with his curiosity, but at the end of that time he found himself standing in front of the innocent sheet of panelling through which the little maid had disappeared. A glance sufficed to show him the position of the secret door – secret, he perceived, only to those who looked with a careless eye. It was just an ordinary door let in flush with the panelling. No latch nor handle betrayed its position, but an unobtrusive catch sunk in the wood invited the thumb. George was astonished that he had not noticed it before; now he had seen it, it was so obvious, almost as obvious as the cupboard door in the library with its lines of imitation shelves and its dummy books. He pulled back the catch and peeped inside.

The staircase, of which the degrees were made not of stone but of blocks of ancient oak, wound up and out of sight. A slit-like window admitted the daylight; he was at the foot of the central tower, and the little window looked out over the terrace; they were still shouting and splashing in the pool below.

'George closed the door and went back to his seat. But his curiosity was not satisfied. Indeed, this partial satisfaction had but whetted its appetite. Where did the staircase lead? What was the errand of the little maid? It was no business of his, he kept repeating – no business of his. He tried to read, but his attention wandered. A quarter-past twelve sounded on the harmonious clock. Suddenly determined, George rose, crossed the room, opened the hidden door, and began to ascend the stairs. He passed the first window, cork-screwed round, and came to another. He paused for a moment to look out; his heart beat uncomfortably, as though he were affronting some unknown danger. What he was doing, he told himself, was extremely ungentlemanly, horribly underbred. He tiptoed onward and upward. One turn more, then half a turn, and a door confronted him. He halted before it, listened; he could hear no sound. Putting his eye to the keyhole, he saw nothing but a stretch of white sunlit wall. Emboldened, he turned the handle and stepped across the threshold. There he halted, petrified by what he saw, mutely gaping.

'In the middle of a pleasantly sunny little room – "it is now Priscilla's boudoir," Mr Wimbush remarked paren-thetically – stood a small circular table of mahogany. Crys-tal, porcelain, and silver, – all the shining apparatus of an elegant meal – were mirrored in its polished depths. The carcase of a cold chicken, a bowl of fruit, a great ham, deeply gashed to its heart of tenderest white and pink, the brown cannon ball of a cold plum-pudding, a slender Hock bottle, and a decanter of claret jostled one another for a place on this festive board. And round the table sat the three sisters, the three lovely Lapiths – eating!

'At George's sudden entrance they had all looked towards the door, and now they sat, petrified by the same astonish-ment which kept George fixed and staring. Georgiana, who sat immediately facing the door, gazed at him with dark, enormous eyes. Between the thumb and forefinger of her right hand she was holding a drumstick of the dismembered chicken; her little finger, elegantly crooked, stood apart from the rest of her hand. Her mouth was open, but the drumstick had never reached its destination; it remained, suspended, frozen, in mid-air. The other two sisters had turned round to look at the intruder. Caroline still grasped her knife and fork; Emmeline's fingers were round the stem of her claret glass. For what seemed a very long time, George and the three sisters stared at one another in silence. They were a group of statues. Then suddenly there was movement. Georgiana dropped her chicken bone, Caroline's knife and fork clattered on her plate. The movement propagated itself, grew more decisive; Emmeline sprang to her feet, uttering a cry. The wave of panic reached George; he turned and, mumbling something unintelligible as he went, rushed out of the room and down the winding stairs. He came to a standstill in the hall, and there, all by himself in the quiet house, he began to laugh.

'At luncheon it was noticed that the sisters ate a little more than usual. Georgiana toyed with some French beans and a spoonful of calves'-foot jelly. "I feel a little stronger to-day," she said to Lord Timpany, when he congratulated her on this increase of appetite; "a little more material," she added, with a nervous laugh. Looking up, she caught George's eye; a blush suffused her cheeks and she looked hastily away.

'In the garden that afternoon they found themselves for a moment alone.

' "You won't tell anyone, George? Promise you won't tell anyone," she implored. "It would make us look so ridiculous. And besides, eating *is* unspiritual, isn't it? Say you won't tell anyone."

' "I will," said George brutally. "I'll tell everyone, unless, . . ."

' "It's blackmail."

' "I don't care," said George. "I'll give you twenty-four hours to decide."

'Lady Lapith was disappointed, of course; she had hoped for better things – for Timpany and a coronet. But George, after all, wasn't so bad. They were married at the New Year.

'My poor grandfather!' Mr Wimbush added, as he closed

his book and put away his pince-nez. 'Whenever I read in the papers about oppressed nationalities, I think of him.' He relighted his cigar. 'It was a maternal government, highly centralized, and there were no representative institutions.'

Henry Wimbush ceased speaking. In the silence that ensued Ivor's whispered commentary on the spirit sketches once more became audible. Priscilla, who had been dozing, suddenly woke up.

'What?' she said in the startled tones of one newly returned to consciousness; 'what?'

Jenny caught the words. She looked up, smiled, nodded reassuringly. 'It's about a ham,' she said.

'What's about a ham?'

'What Henry has been reading.' She closed the red notebook lying on her knees and slipped a rubber hand round it. 'I'm going to bed,' she announced, and got up.

'So am I,' said Anne, yawning. But she lacked the energy to rise from her arm-chair.

The night was hot and oppressive. Round the open windows the curtains hung unmoving. Ivor, fanning himself with the portrait of an Astral Being, looked out into the darkness and drew a breath.

'The air's like wool,' he declared.

'It will get cooler after midnight,' said Henry Wimbush, and cautiously added, 'perhaps.'

'I shan't sleep, I know.'

Priscilla turned her head in his direction; the monumental coiffure nodded exorbitantly at her slightest movement. 'You must make an effort,' she said. 'When I can't sleep, I concentrate my will: I say, "I will sleep, I am asleep!" And pop! off I go. That's the power of thought.'

'But does it work on stuffy nights?' Ivor inquired. 'I simply cannot sleep on a stuffy night.'

'Nor can I,' said Mary, 'except out of doors.'

'Out of doors! What a wonderful idea!' In the end they decided to sleep on the towers – Mary on the western tower, Ivor on the eastern. There was a flat expanse of leads on each of the towers, and you could get a mattress through the trap doors that opened on to them. Under the stars, under the gibbous moon, assuredly they would sleep. The mattresses were hauled up, sheets and blankets were spread, and an hour later the two insomniasts, each on his separate tower, were crying their good-nights across the dividing gulf.

On Mary the sleep-compelling charm of the open air did not work with its expected magic. Even through the mattress one could not fail to be aware that the leads were extremely hard. Then there were noises : the owls screeched tirelessly, and once, roused by some unknown terror, all the geese of the farmyard burst into a sudden frenzy of cackling. The stars and the gibbous moon demanded to be looked at, and when one meteorite had streaked across the sky, you could not help waiting, open-eyed and alert, for the next. Time passed; the moon climbed higher and higher in the sky. Mary felt less sleepy than she had when she first came out. She sat up and looked over the parapet. Had Ivor been able to sleep? she wondered. And as though in answer to her mental question, from behind the chimney-stack at the farther end of the roof a white form noiselessly emerged – a form that, in the moonlight, was recognizably Ivor's. Spreading his arms to right and left, like a tight-rope dancer, he began to walk forward along the roof-tree of the house. He swayed terrifyingly as he advanced. Mary looked on speechlessly; perhaps he was walking in his sleep ! Suppose he were to wake up suddenly, now ! If she spoke or moved it might mean his death. She dared look no more, but sank back on her pillows. She listened intently. For what seemed an immensely long time there was no sound. Then there was a patter of feet on the tiles, followed by a scrabbling noise and a whispered 'Damn !' And suddenly Ivor's head and shoulders appeared above the parapet. One leg followed, then the other. He was on the leads. Mary pretended to wake up with a start.

'Oh !' she said. 'What are you doing here?'

'I couldn't sleep,' he explained, 'so I came along to see if you couldn't. One gets bored by oneself on a tower. Don't you find it so?'

It was light before five. Long, narrow clouds barred the east, their edges bright with orange fire. The sky was pale and watery. With the mournful scream of a soul in pain, a monstrous peacock, flying heavily up from below, alighted on the parapet of the tower. Ivor and Mary started broad awake.

'Catch him!' cried Ivor, jumping up. 'We'll have a feather.' The frightened peacock ran up and down the parapet in an absurd distress, curtseying and bobbing and clucking; his long tail swung ponderously back and forth as he turned and turned again. Then with a flap and swish he launched himself upon the air and sailed magnificently earthward, with a recovered dignity. But he had left a trophy. Ivor had his feather, a long-lashed eye of purple and green, of blue and gold. He handed it to his companion.

'An angel's feather,' he said.

Mary looked at it for a moment, gravely and intently. Her purple pyjamas clothed her with an ampleness that hid the lines of her body; she looked like some large, comfortable, unjointed toy, a sort of Teddy bear – but a Teddy bear with an angel's head, pink cheeks, and hair like a bell of gold. An angel's face, the feather of an angel's wing. . . . Somehow the whole atmosphere of this sunrise was rather angelic.

'It's extraordinary to think of sexual selection,' she said at last, looking up from her contemplation of the miraculous feather.

'Extraordinary!' Ivor echoed. 'I select you, you select me. What luck!'

He put his arm round her shoulders and they stood looking eastward. The first sunlight had begun to warm and colour the pale light of the dawn. Mauve pyjamas and white pyjamas; they were a young and charming couple. The rising sun touched their faces. It was all extremely symbolic; but then, if you choose to think so, nothing in this world is not symbolical. Profound and beautiful truth!

'I must be getting back to my tower,' said Ivor at last.

'Already?'

'I'm afraid so. The varletry will soon be up and about.'

'Ivor. . . .' There was a prolonged and silent farewell.

'And now,' said Ivor, 'I repeat my tight-rope stunt.'

Mary threw her arms round his neck. 'You mustn't, Ivor. It's dangerous. Please.'

He had to yield at last to her entreaties. 'All right,' he said, 'I'll go down through the house and up at the other end.'

He vanished through the trap door into the darkness that

still lurked within the shuttered house. A minute later he had reappeared on the farther tower; he waved his hand, and then sank down, out of sight, behind the parapet. From below, in the house, came the thin wasp-like buzzing of an alarum-clock. He had gone back just in time.

CHAPTER XX

Ivor was gone. Lounging behind the wind-screen in his yellow sedan he was whirling across rural England. Social and amorous engagements of the most urgent character called him from hall to baronial hall, from castle to castle, from Elizabethan manor-house to Georgian mansion, over the whole expanse of the kingdom. Today in Somerset, to-morrow in Warwickshire, on Saturday in the West Riding, by Tuesday morning in Argyll – Ivor never rested. The whole summer through, from the beginning of July till the end of September, he devoted himself to his engagements; he was a martyr to them. In the autumn he went back to London for a holiday. Crome had been a little incident, an evanescent bubble on the stream of his life; it belonged already to the past. By tea-time he would be at Gobley, and there would be Zenobia's welcoming smile. And on Thursday morning – but that was a long, long way ahead. He would think of Thursday morning when Thursday morning arrived. Meanwhile there was Gobley, meanwhile Zenobia.

In the visitors' book at Crome Ivor had left, according to his invariable custom in these cases, a poem. He had im-provised it magisterially in the ten minutes preceding his departure. Denis and Mr Scogan strolled back together from the gates of the courtyard, whence they had bidden their last farewells; on the writing-table in the hall they found the visitors' book, open, and Ivor's composition scarcely dry. Mr Scogan read it aloud :

'The magic of those immemorial kings,
  Who webbed enchantment on the bowls of night,
Sleeps in the soul of all created things;
  In the blue sea, th' Acroceraunian height,
In the eyed butterfly's auricular wings
  And orgied visions of the anchorite;
In all that singing flies and flying sings,
  In rain, in pain, in delicate delight.
But much more magic, much more cogent spells

Weave here their wizardries about my soul.
Crome calls me like the voice of vesperal bells,
Haunts like a ghostly-peopled necropole.
  Fate tears me hence. Hard fate! since far from Crome
  My soul must weep, remembering its Home.'

'Very nice and tasteful and tactful,' said Mr Scogan,
when he had finished. 'I am only troubled by the butterfly's
auricular wings. You had a first-hand knowledge of the
workings of a poet's mind, Denis; perhaps you can explain.'

'What could be simpler,' said Denis. 'It's a beautiful word,
and Ivor wanted to say that the wings were golden.'

'You make it luminously clear.'

'One suffers so much,' Denis went on, 'from the fact
that beautiful words don't always mean what they ought to
mean. Recently, for example, I had a whole poem ruined,
just because the word "carminative" didn't mean what it
ought to have meant. Carminative – it's admirable, isn't it?'

'Admirable,' Mr Scogan agreed. 'And what does it mean?'

'It's a word I've treasured from my earliest infancy,' said
Denis, 'treasured and loved. They used to give me cinnamon
when I had a cold – quite useless, but not disagreeable. One
poured it drop by drop out of narrow bottles, a golden
liquor, fierce and fiery. On the label was a list of its virtues,
and among other things it was described as being in the
highest degree carminative. I adored the word. "Isn't it
carminative?" I used to say to myself when I'd taken my
dose. It seemed so wonderfully to describe that sensation of
internal warmth, that glow, that – what shall I call it? –
physical self-satisfaction which followed the drinking of cinnamon. Later, when I discovered alcohol, "carminative"
described for me that similar, but nobler, more spiritual
glow which wine evokes not only in the body but in the
soul as well. The carminative virtues of burgundy, of rum,
of old brandy, of Lacryma Christi, of Marsala, of Aleatico,
of stout, of gin, of champagne, of claret, of the raw new
wine of this year's Tuscan vintage – I compared them. I
classified them. Marsala is rosily, downily carminative; gin
pricks and refreshes while it warms. I had a whole table of
carmination values. And now' – Denis spread out his hands,

palm upwards, despairingly – 'Now I know what carminative really means.'

'Well, what *does* it mean?' asked Mr Scogan, a little impatiently.

'Carminative,' said Denis, lingering lovingly over the syllables, 'carminative. I imagined vaguely that it had something to do with *carmen-carminis*, still more vaguely with *caro-carnis*, and its derivatives, like carnival and carnation. Carminative – there was the idea of singing and the idea of flesh, rose-coloured and warm, with a suggestion of the jollities of mi-Carême and the masked holidays of Venice. Carminative – the warmth, the glow, the interior ripeness were all in the word. Instead of which...'

'Do come to the point, my dear Denis,' protested Mr Scogan. 'Do come to the point.'

'Well, I wrote a poem the other day,' said Denis; 'I wrote a poem about the effects of love.'

'Others have done the same before you,' said Mr Scogan. 'There is no need to be ashamed.'

'I was putting forward the notion,' Denis went on, 'that the effects of love were often similar to the effects of wine, that Eros would intoxicate as well as Bacchus. Love, for example, is essentially carminative. It gives one the sense of warmth, the glow.

"And passion carminative as wine ..."

was what I wrote. Not only was the line elegantly sonorous; it was also, I flattered myself, very aptly and compendiously expressive. Everything was in the word carminative – a detailed, exact foreground, an immense, indefinite hinterland of suggestion.

"And passion carminative as wine ..."

I was not ill-pleased. And then suddenly it occurred to me that I had never actually looked up the word in a dictionary. Carminative had grown up with me from the days of the cinnamon bottle. It had always been taken for granted. Carminative: for me the word was as rich in content as some tremendous, elaborate work of art; it was a complete landscape with figures.

It was the first time I had ever committed the word to writing, and all at once I felt I would like lexicographical authority for it. A small English-German dictionary was all I had at hand. I turned up C, ca, car, carm. There it was: "Carminative: *windtreibend.*" *Windtreibend!*' he repeated. Mr Scogan laughed. Denis shook his head. 'Ah,' he said, 'for me it was no laughing matter. For me it marked the end of a chapter, the death of something young and precious. There were the years – years of childhood and innocence – when I had believed that carminative meant – well, carminative. And now, before me lies the rest of my life – a day, perhaps, ten years, half a century, when I shall know that carminative means *windtriebend.*

> "Plus ne suis ce que j'ai été
> Et ne le saurai jamais être."

It is a realization that makes one rather melancholy.'

'Carminative,' said Mr Scogan thoughtfully.

'Carminative,' Denis repeated, and they were silent for a time. 'Words,' said Denis at last, 'words – I wonder if you can realize how much I love them. You are too much pre-occupied with mere things and ideas and people to under-stand the full beauty of words. Your mind is not a literary mind. The spectacle of Mr Gladstone finding thirty-four rhymes to the name "Margot" seems to you rather pathetic than anything else. Mallarmés envelopes with their versified addresses leave you cold, unless they leave you pitiful; you can't see that

> "Apte à ne point te cabrer, hue !
> Poste, et j'ajouterai, dia !
> Si tu ne fuis onze-bis Rue
> Balzac, chez cet Heredia,"

is a little miracle.'

'You're right,' said Mr Scogan. 'I can't.'

'You don't feel it to be magical?'

'No.'

'That's the test for the literary mind,' said Denis; 'the feeling of magic, the sense that words have power. The technical, verbal part of literature is simply a development of magic. Words are man's first and most grandiose invention. With language, he created a whole new universe; what wonder if he loved words and attributed power to them! With fitted, harmonious words the magicians summoned rabbits out of empty hats and spirits from the elements. Their descendants, the literary men, still go on with the process, morticing their verbal formulas together and, before the power of the finished spell, trembling with delight and awe. Rabbits out of empty hats? No, their spells are more subtly powerful, for they evoke emotions out of empty minds. Formulated by their art, the most insipid statements become enormously significant. For example, I proffer the constatation, "Black ladders lack bladders." A self-evident truth, one on which it would not have been worth while to insist, had I chosen to formulate it in such words as "Black fire-escapes have no bladders," or, "Les échelles noires manquent de vessie." But since I put it as I do, "Black ladders lack bladders," it becomes, for all its self-evidence, significant, unforgettable, moving. The creation by word-power of something out of nothing – what is that but magic? And, I may add, what is that but literature? Half the world's greatest poetry is simply "Les échelles noires manquent de vessie," translated into magic significance as, "Black ladders lack bladders." And you can't appreciate words. I'm sorry for you.'

'A mental carminative,' said Mr Scogan reflectively. 'That's what you need.'

CHAPTER XXI

Perched on its four stone mushrooms, the little granary stood two or three feet above the grass of the green close. Beneath it there was a perpetual shade and a damp growth of long, luxuriant grasses. Here, in the shadow, in the green dampness, a family of white ducks had sought shelter from the afternoon sun. Some stood, preening themselves, some reposed with their long bellies pressed to the ground, as though the cool grass were water. Little social noises burst fitfully forth, and from time to time some pointed tail would execute a brilliant Lisztian tremolo. Suddenly their jovial repose was shattered. A prodigious thump shook the wooden flooring above their heads; the whole granary trembled, little fragments of dirt and crumbled wood rained down among them. With a loud, continuous quacking the ducks rushed out from beneath this nameless menace, and did not stay their flight till they were safely in the farmyard.

'Don't lose your temper,' Anne was saying. 'Listen! You've frightened the ducks. Poor dears! no wonder.' She was sitting sideways in a low, wooden chair. Her right elbow rested on the back of the chair and she supported her cheek on her hand. Her long, slender body drooped into curves of a lazy grace. She was smiling, and she looked at Gombauld through half-closed eyes.

'Damn you!' Gombauld repeated, and stamped his foot again. He glared at her round the half-finished portrait on the easel.

'Poor ducks!' Anne repeated. The sound of their quacking was faint in the distance; it was inaudible.

'Can't you see you make me lose my time?' he asked. 'I can't work with you dangling about distractingly like this.'

'You'd lose less time if you stopped talking and stamping your feet and did a little painting for a change. After all, what am I dangling about for, except to be painted?'

Gombauld made a noise like a growl. 'You're awful,' he said, with conviction. 'Why do you ask me to come and stay here? Why do you tell me you'd like me to paint your portrait?'

'For the simple reasons that I like you – at least, when you're in a good temper – and that I think you're a good painter.'

'For the simple reason' – Gombauld mimicked her voice – 'that you want me to make love to you and, when I do, to have the amusement of running away.'

Anne threw back her head and laughed. 'So you think it amuses me to have to evade your advances! So like a man! If only you knew how gross and awful and boring men are when they try to make love and you don't want them to make love! If you could only see yourselves through our eyes!'

Gombauld picked up his palette and brushes and attacked his canvas with the ardour of irritation. 'I suppose you'll be saying next that you didn't start the game, that it was I who made the first advances, and that you were the innocent victim who sat still and never did anything that could invite or allure me on.'

'So like a man again!' said Anne. 'It's always the same old story about the woman tempting the man. The woman lures, fascinates, invites; and man – noble man, innocent man – falls a victim. My poor Gombauld! Surely you're not going to sing that old song again. It's so unintelligent, and I always thought you were a man of sense.'

'Thanks,' said Gombauld.

'Be a little objective,' Anne went on. 'Can't you see that you're simply externalizing your own emotions? That's what you men are always doing; it's so barbarously naïve. You feel one of your loose desires for some woman, and because you desire her strongly you immediately accuse her of luring you on, of deliberately provoking and inviting the desire. You have the mentality of savages. You might just as well say that a plate of strawberries and cream deliberately lures you on to feel greedy. In ninety-nine cases out of a hundred women are as passive and innocent as the strawberries and cream.'

'Well, all I can say is that this must be the hundredth case,' said Gombauld, without looking up.

Anne shrugged her shoulders and gave vent to a sigh. 'I'm at a loss to know whether you're more silly or more rude.'

After painting for a little time in silence Gombauld began to speak again. 'And then there's Denis,' he said, renewing the conversation as though it had only just been broken off. 'You're playing the same game with him. Why can't you leave that wretched young man in peace?'

Anne flushed with a sudden and uncontrollable anger. 'It's perfectly untrue about Denis,' she said indignantly. 'I never dreamt of playing what you beautifully call the same game with him.' Recovering her calm, she added in her ordinary cooing voice and with her exacerbating smile, 'You've become very protective towards poor Denis all of a sudden.'

'I have,' Gombauld replied, with a gravity that was somehow a little too solemn. 'I don't like to see a young man . . .'

'. . . being whirled along the road to ruin,' said Anne, continuing his sentence for him. 'I admire your sentiments and, believe me, I share them.'

She was curiously irritated at what Gombauld had said about Denis. It happened to be so completely untrue. Gombauld might have some slight ground for his reproaches. But Denis – no, she had never flirted with Denis. Poor boy! He was very sweet. She became somewhat pensive.

Gombauld painted on with fury. The restlessness of an unsatisfied desire, which, before, had distracted his mind, making work impossible, seemed now to have converted itself into a kind of feverish energy. When it was finished, he told himself, the portrait would be diabolic. He was painting her in the pose she had naturally adopted at the first sitting. Seated sideways, her elbow on the back of the chair, her head and shoulders turned at an angle from the rest of her body, towards the front, she had fallen into an attitude of indolent abandonment. He had emphasized the lazy curves of her body; the lines sagged as they crossed the canvas, the grace of the painted figure seemed to be melting into a kind of soft decay. The hand that lay along the knee was as limp as a glove. He was at work on the face now; it had begun to emerge on the canvas, doll-like in its regularity and listlessness. It was Anne's face – but her face as it would be, utterly unillumined by the inward lights of thought and emotion. It was the lazy, expressionless mask which was sometimes her face. The portrait was terribly like; and at the same time it was the most malicious of lies. Yes, it would be diabolic when it was finished, Gombauld decided; he wondered what she would think of it.

CHAPTER XXII

For the sake of peace and quiet Denis had retired earlier on this same afternoon to his bedroom. He wanted to work, but the hour was a drowsy one, and lunch, so recently eaten, weighed heavily on body and mind. The meridian demon was upon him; he was possessed by that bored and hopeless post-prandial melancholy which the coenobites of old knew and feared under the name of 'accidie.' He felt, like Ernest Dowson, 'a little weary.' He was in the mood to write something rather exquisite and gentle and quietist in tone; something a little droopy and at the same time – how should he put it? – a little infinite. He though of Anne, of love hopeless and unattainable. Perhaps that was the ideal kind of love, the hopeless kind – the quiet, theoretical kind of love. In this sad mood of repletion he could well believe it. He began to write. One elegant quatrain had flowed from beneath his pen :

> 'A brooding love which is at most
>   The stealth of moonbeams when they slide,
>   Evoking colour's bloodless ghost,
>   O'er some scarce-breathing breast or side ...'

when his attention was attracted by a sound from outside. He looked down from his window; there they were, Anne and Gombauld, talking, laughing together. They crossed the courtyard in front, and passed out of sight through the gate in the right-hand wall. That was the way to the green close and the granary; she was going to sit for him again. His pleasantly depressing melancholy was dissipated by a puff of violent emotion; angrily he threw his quatrain into the waste-paper basket and ran downstairs. 'The stealth of moonbeams,' indeed !

In the hall he saw Mr Scogan; the man seemed to be lying in wait. Denis tried to escape, but in vain. Mr Scogan's eye glittered like the eye of the Ancient Mariner.

'Not so fast,' he said,' stretching out a small saurian hand with pointed nails – 'not so fast. I was just going down to the flower garden to take the sun. We'll go together.'

Denis abandoned himself; Mr Scogan put on his hat and they went out arm in arm. On the shaven turf of the terrace Henry Wimbush and Mary were playing a solemn game of bowls. They descended by the yew-tree walk. It was here, thought Denis, here that Anne had fallen, here that he had kissed her, here – and he blushed with retrospective shame at the memory – here that he had tried to carry her and failed. Life was awful!

'Sanity!' said Mr Scogan, suddenly breaking a long silence. 'Sanity – that's what's wrong with me and that's what will be wrong with you, my dear Denis, when you're old enough to be sane or insane. In a sane world I should be a great man; as things are, in this curious establishment, I am nothing at all; to all intents and purposes I don't exist. I am just *Vox et praeterea nihil*.'

Denis made no response; he was thinking of other things. 'After all,' he said to himself – 'after all, Gombauld is better looking than I, more entertaining, more confident; and, besides, he's already somebody and I'm still only potential. . . .'

'Everything that ever gets done in this world is done by madmen,' Mr Scogan went on. Denis tried not to listen, but the tireless insistence of Mr Scogan's discourse gradually compelled his attention. 'Men such as I am, such as you may possibly become, have never achieved anything. We're too sane; we're merely reasonable. We lack the human touch, the compelling enthusiastic mania. People are quite ready to listen to the philosophers for a little amusement, just as they would listen to a fiddler or a mountebank. But as to acting on the advice of the men of reason – never. Wherever the choice has had to be made between the man of reason and the madman, the world has unhesitatingly followed the madman. For the madman appeals to what is fundamental, to passion and the instincts; the philosophers to what is superficial and supererogatory – reason.'

They entered the garden; at the head of one of the alleys stood a green wooden bench, embayed in the midst of a fragrant continent of lavender bushes. It was here, though the place was shadeless and one breathed hot, dry perfume instead of air – it was here that Mr Scogan elected to sit. He thrived on untempered sunlight.

'Consider, for example, the case of Luther and Erasmus.' He took out his pipe and began to fill it as he talked. 'There was Erasmus, a man of reason if ever there was one. People listened to him at first – a new virtuoso performing on that elegant and resourceful instrument, the intellect; they even admired and venerated him. But did he move them to behave as he wanted them to behave – reasonably, decently, or at least a little less porkishly than usual? He did not. And then Luther appears, violent, passionate, a madman insanely convinced about matters in which there can be no conviction. He shouted, and men rushed to follow him. Erasmus was no longer listened to; he was reviled for his reasonableness. Luther was serious, Luther was reality – like the Great War. Erasmus was only reason and decency; he lacked the power, being a sage, to move men to action. Europe followed Luther and embarked on a century and a half of war and bloody persecution. It's a melancholy story.' Mr Scogan lighted a match. In the intense light the flame was all but invisible. The smell of burning tobacco began to mingle with the sweetly acrid smell of the lavender.

'If you want to get men to act reasonably, you must set about persuading them in a maniacal manner. The very sane precepts of the founders of religions are only made infectious by means of enthusiasms which to a sane man must appear deplorable. It is humiliating to find how impotent unadulterated sanity is. Sanity, for example, informs us that the only way in which we can preserve civilization is by behaving decently and intelligently. Sanity appeals and argues; our rulers persevere in their customary porkishness, while we acquiesce and obey. The only hope is a maniacal crusade; I am ready, when it comes, to beat a tambourine with the loudest, but at the same time I shall feel a little ashamed of myself. However' – Mr Scogan shrugged his shoulders and, pipe in hand, made a gesture of resignation – 'it's futile to complain that things are as they are. The fact remains that sanity unassisted is useless. What we want, then, is a sane and reasonable exploitation of the forces of insanity. We sane men will have the power yet.' Mr Scogan's eyes shone with a more than ordinary brightness, and, taking his pipe out of his mouth, he gave vent to his loud, dry, and somehow rather fiendish laugh.

'But I don't want power,' said Denis. He was sitting in limp discomfort at one end of the bench, shading his eyes from the intolerable light. Mr Scogan, bolt upright at the other end, laughed again.

'Everybody wants power,' he said. 'Power in some form or other. The sort of power you hanker for is literary power. Some people want power to persecute other human beings; you expend your lust for power in persecuting words, twisting them, moulding them, torturing them to obey you. But I divagate.'

'Do you?' asked Denis faintly.

'Yes,' Mr Scogan continued, unheeding, 'the time will come. We men of intelligence will learn to harness the insanities to the service of reason. We can't leave the world any longer to the direction of chance. We can't allow dangerous maniacs like Luther, mad about dogma, like Napoleon, mad about himself, to go on casually appearing and turning everything upside-down. In the past it didn't so much matter; but our modern machine is too delicate. A few more knocks like the Great War, another Luther or two, and the whole concern will go to pieces. In future, the men of reason must see that the madness of the world's maniacs is canalized into proper channels, is made to do useful work, like a mountain torrent driving a dynamo. . . .'

'Making electricity to light a Swiss hotel,' said Denis. 'You ought to complete the simile.'

Mr Scogan waved away the interruption. 'There's only one thing to be done,' he said. 'The men of intelligence must combine, must conspire, and seize power from the imbeciles and maniacs who now direct us. They must found the Rational State.'

The heat that was slowly paralysing all Denis's mental and bodily faculties seemed to bring to Mr Scogan additional vitality. He talked with an ever-increasing energy, his hands moved in sharp, quick, precise gestures, his eyes shone. Hard, dry, and continuous, his voice went on sounding and sounding in Denis's ears with the insistence of a mechanical noise.

'In the Rational State,' he heard Mr Scogan saying, 'human beings will be separated out into distinct species, not according to the colour of their eyes or the shape of their skulls, but according to the qualities of their mind and temperament. Examining psychologists, trained to what would now seem an almost superhuman clairvoyance, will test each child that is born and assign it to its proper species. Duly labelled and docketed, the child will be given the education suitable to members of its species, and will be set, in adult life, to perform those functions which human beings of his variety are capable of performing.'

'How many species will there be?' asked Denis.

'A great many, no doubt,' Mr Scogan answered; 'the classification will be subtle and elaborate. But it is not in the power of a prophet to go into details, nor is it his business. I will do no more than indicate the three main species into which the subjects of the Rational State will be divided.'

He paused, cleared his throat, and coughed once or twice, evoking in Denis's mind the vision of a table with a glass and water-bottle, and, lying across one corner, a long white pointer for the lantern pictures.

'The three main species,' Mr Scogan went on, 'will be these : the Directing Intelligences, the Men of Faith, and the Herd. Among the Intelligences will be found all those capable of thought, those who knew how to attain to a certain degree of freedom – and, alas, how limited, even among the most intelligent, that freedom is ! – from the mental bondage of their time. A select body of Intelligences, drawn from among those who have turned their attention to the problems of practical life, will be the governors of the Rational State. They will employ as their instruments of power the second great species of humanity – the men of Faith, the Madmen, as I have been calling them, who believe in things unreasonably, with passion, and are ready to die for their beliefs and their desires. These wild men, with their fearful potentialities for good or for mischief, will no longer be allowed to react casually to a casual environment. There will be no more Caesar Borgias, no more Luthers and Mohammeds, no more Joanna Southcotts, no more Comstocks. The old-fashioned Man of Faith and Desire, that haphazard creature of brute circumstance, who might drive men to tears and repentance, or who might equally well set them on to cutting one another's throats, will be replaced by a new sort of madman, still externally the same, still bubbling with a seemingly spontaneous enthusiasm, but, ah, how very different from the madman of the past ! For the new Man of Faith will be expending his passion, his desire, and his enthusiasm in the propagation of some reasonable idea. He will be, all unawares, the tool of some superior intelligence.'

Mr Scogan chuckled maliciously; it was as though he were taking a revenge, in the name of reason, on the enthusiasts. 'From their earliest years, as soon, that is, as the examining psychologists have assigned them their place in the classified scheme, the Men of Faith will have had their special education under the eye of the Intelligences. Moulded by a long process of suggestion, they will go out into the world, preaching and practising with a generous mania the coldly reasonable projects of the Directors from above. When these projects are accomplished, or when the ideas that were useful a decade ago have ceased to be useful, the Intelligences will inspire a new generation of madmen with a new eternal truth. The principal function of the Men of Faith will be to move and direct the Multitude, that third great species consisting of those countless millions who lack intelligence and are without valuable enthusiasm. When any particular effort is required of the Herd, when it is thought necessary, for the sake of solidarity, that humanity shall be kindled and united by some single enthusiastic desire or idea, the Men of Faith, primed with some simple and satisfying creed, will be sent out on a mission of evangelization. At ordinary times, when the high spiritual temperature of a Crusade would be unhealthy, the Men of Faith will be quietly and earnestly busy with the great work of education. In the upbringing of the Herd, humanity's almost boundless suggestibility will be scientifically exploited. Systematically, from earliest infancy, its members will be assured that there is no happiness to be found except in work and obedience; they will be made to believe that they are happy, that they are tremendously important beings, and that everything they do is noble and significant. For the lower species the earth will be restored to the centre of the universe and man to pre-eminence on the earth. Oh, I envy the lot of the commonalty in the Rational State ! Working their eight hours a day, obeying their betters, convinced of their own

grandeur and significance and immortality, they will be marvellously happy, happier than any race of men has ever
been. They will go through life in a rosy state of intoxication,
from which they will never awake. The Men of Faith will
play the cup-bearers at this lifelong bacchanal, filling and
ever filling again with the warm liquor that the Intelligences,
in sad and sober privacy behind the scenes, will brew for the
intoxication of their subjects.'

'And what will be my place in the Rational State?' Denis
drowsily inquired from under his shading hand.

Mr Scogan looked at him for a moment in silence. 'It's
difficult to see where you would fit in,' he said at last. 'You
couldn't do manual work; you're too independent and un-
suggestible to belong to the larger Herd; you have none of
the characteristics required in a Man of Faith. As for the
Directing Intelligences, they will have to be marvellously
clear and merciless and penetrating.' He paused and shook
his head. 'No, I can see no place for you; only the lethal
chamber.'

Deeply hurt, Denis emitted the imitation of a loud
Homeric laugh. 'I'm getting sunstroke here,' he said, and
got up.

Mr Scogan followed his example, and they walked slowly
away down the narrow path, brushing the blue lavender
flowers in their passage. Denis pulled a sprig of lavender and
sniffed at it; then some dark leaves of rosemary that smelt
like incense in a cavernous church. They passed a bed of
opium poppies, dispetaled now; the round, ripe seed-heads
were brown and dry – like Polynesian trophies, Denis
thought; severed heads stuck on poles. He liked the fancy
enough to impart it to Mr Scogan.

'Like Polynesian trophies. . . .' Uttered aloud, the fancy
seemed less charming and significant that it did when it first
occurred to him.

There was a silence, and in a growing wave of sound the
whir of the reaping machines swelled up from the fields
beyond the garden and then receded into a remoter hum.

'It is satisfactory to think,' said Mr Scogan, as they strolled
slowly onward, 'that a multitude of people are toiling in the
harvest fields in order that we may talk of Polynesia. Like
every other good thing in this world, leisure and culture

have to be paid for. Fortunately, however, it is not the leisured and the cultured who have to pay. Let us be duly thankful for that, my dear Denis – duly thankful,' he repeated, and knocked the ashes out of his pipe.

Denis was not listening. He had suddenly remembered Anne. She was with Gombauld – alone with him in his studio. It was an intolerable thought.

'Shall we go and pay a call on Gombauld?' he suggested carelessly. 'It would be amusing to see what he's doing now.'

He laughed inwardly to think how furious Gombauld would be when he saw them arriving.

CHAPTER XXIII

Gombauld was by no means so furious at their apparition as Denis had hoped and expected he would be. Indeed, he was rather pleased than annoyed when the two faces, one brown and pointed, the other round and pale, appeared in the frame of the open door. The energy born of his restless irritation was dying within him, returning to its emotional elements. A moment more and he would have been losing his temper again – and Anne would be keeping hers, infuriatingly. Yes, he was positively glad to see them.

'Come in, come in,' he called out hospitably.

Followed by Mr Scogan, Denis climbed the little ladder and stepped over the threshold. He looked suspiciously from Gombauld to his sitter, and could learn nothing from the expression of their faces except that they both seemed pleased to see the visitors. Were they really glad, or were they cunningly simulating gladness? He wondered.

Mr Scogan, meanwhile, was looking at the portrait.

'Excellent,' he said approvingly, 'excellent. Almost too true to character, if that is possible; yes, positively too true. But I'm surprised to find you putting in all this psychology business.' He pointed to the face, and with his extended finger followed the slack curves of the painted figure. 'I thought you were one of the fellows who went in exclusively for balanced masses and impinging planes.'

Gombauld laughed. 'This is a little infidelity,' he said.

'I'm sorry,' said Mr Scogan. 'I for one, without ever having had the slightest appreciation of painting, have always taken particular pleasure in Cubismus. I like to see pictures from which nature has been completely banished, pictures which are exclusively the product of the human mind. They give me the same pleasure as I derive from a good piece of reasoning or a mathematical problem or an achievement of engineering. Nature, or anything that reminds me of nature, disturbs me; it is too large, too complicated, above all too utterly pointless and incomprehensible. I am at home with the works of man; if I choose to set my mind to it, I can understand anything that any man has made or thought. That is why I always travel by Tube, never by bus if I can possibly help it. For, travelling by bus, one can't avoid seeing, even in London, a few stray works of God – the sky, for example, an occasional tree, the flowers in the window-boxes. But travel by Tube and you see nothing but the works of man – iron riveted into geometrical forms, straight lines of concrete, patterned expanses of tiles. All is human and the product of friendly and comprehensible minds. All philosophies and all religions – what are they but spiritual Tubes bored through the universe ! Through these narrow tunnels, where all is recognizably human, one travels comfortable and secure, contriving to forget that all round and below and above them stretches the blind mass of earth, endless and unexplored. Yes, give me the Tube and Cubismus every time; give me ideas, so snug and neat and simple and well made. And preserve me from nature, preserve me from all that's inhumanly large and complicated and obscure. I haven't the courage, and, above all, I haven't the time to start wandering in that labyrinth.'

While Mr Scogan was discoursing, Denis had crossed over to the farther side of the little square chamber, where Anne was sitting, still in her graceful, lazy pose, on the low chair.

'Well?' he demanded, looking at her almost fiercely. What was he asking of her? He hardly knew himself.

Anne looked up at him, and for answer echoed his 'Well?' in another, a laughing key.

Denis had nothing more, at the moment, to say. Two or three canvases stood in the corner behind Anne's chair, their faces turned to the wall. He pulled them out and began to look at the paintings.

'May I see too?' Anne requested.

He stood them in a row against the wall. Anne had to turn round in her chair to look at them. There was the big canvas of the man fallen from the horse, there was a painting of flowers, there was a small landscape. His hands on the back of the chair, Denis leaned over her. From behind the easel at the other side of the room Mr Scogan was talking away. For a long time they looked at the pictures, saying nothing; or, rather, Anne looked at the pictures, while Denis, for the most part, looked at Anne.

'I like the man and the horse; don't you?' she said at last, looking up with an inquiring smile.

Denis nodded, and then in a queer, strangled voice, as though it had cost him a great effort to utter the words, he said, 'I love you.'

It was a remark which Anne had heard a good many times before and mostly heard with equanimity. But on this occasion – perhaps because they had come so unexpectedly, perhaps for some other reason – the words provoked in her a certain surprised commotion.

'My poor Denis,' she managed to say, with a laugh; but she was blushing as she spoke.

CHAPTER XXIV

It was noon. Denis, descending from his chamber, where he had been making an unsuccessful effort to write something about nothing in particular, found the drawing-room deserted. He was about to go out into the garden when his eye fell on a familiar but mysterious object – the large red notebook in which he had so often seen Jenny quietly and busily scribbling. She had left it lying on the window-seat. The temptation was great. He picked up the book and slipped off the elastic band that kept it discreetly closed.

'Private. Not to be opened,' was written in capital letters on the cover. He raised his eyebrows. It was the sort of thing one wrote in one's Latin Grammar while one was still at one's preparatory school.

'Black is the raven, black is the rook,
But blacker the thief who steals this book !'

It was curiously childish, he thought, and he smiled to himself. He opened the book. What he saw made him wince as though he had been struck.

Denis was his own severest critic; so, at least, he had always believed. He liked to think of himself as a merciless vivisector probing into the palpitating entrails of his own soul; he was Brown Dog to himself. His weaknesses, his absurdities – no one knew them better than he did. Indeed in a vague way he imagined that nobody beside himself was aware of them at all. It seemed, somehow, inconceivable that he should appear to other people as they appeared to him, inconceivable that they ever spoke of him among themselves in that same freely critical and, to be quite honest, mildly malicious tone in which he was accustomed to talk of them. In his own eyes he had defects, but to see them was a privilege reserved to him alone. For the rest of the world he was surely an image of flawless crystal. It was almost axiomatic.

On opening the red notebook that crystal image of himself crashed to the ground, and was irreparably shattered.

He was not his own severest critic after all. The discovery was a painful one.

The fruit of Jenny's unobtrusive scribbling lay before him. A caricature of himself, reading (the book was upside-down). In the background a dancing couple, recognizable as Gombauld and Anne. Beneath, the legend : 'Fable of the Wallflower and the Sour Grapes.' Fascinated and horrified, Denis pored over the drawing. It was masterful. A mute, inglorious Rouveyre appeared in every one of those cruelly clear lines. The expression of the face, an assumed aloofness and superiority tempered by a feeble envy; the attitude of the body and limbs, an attitude of studious and scholarly dignity, given away by the fidgety pose of the turned-in feet – these things were terrible. And, more terrible still, was the likeness, was the magisterial certainty with which his physical peculiarities were all recorded and subtly exaggerated.

Denis looked deeper into the book. There were caricatures of other people : of Priscilla and Mr Barbecue-Smith; of Henry Wimbush, of Anne and Gombauld; of Mr Scogan, whom Jenny had represented in a light that was more than slightly sinister, that was, indeed, diabolic; of Mary and Ivor. He scarcely glanced at them. A fearful desire to know the worst about himself possessed him. He turned over the leaves, lingering at nothing that was not his own image. Seven full pages were devoted to him.

'Private. Not to be opened.' He had disobeyed the injunction; he had only got what he deserved. Thoughtfully he closed the book, and slid the rubber band once more into its place. Sadder and wiser, he went out on to the terrace. And so this, he reflected, this was how Jenny employed the leisure hours in her ivory tower apart. And he had thought her a simple-minded, uncritical creature ! It was he, it seemed, who was the fool. He felt no resentment towards Jenny. No, the distressing thing wasn't Jenny herself; it was what she and the phenomenon of her red book represented, what they stood for and concretely symbolized. They represented all the vast conscious world of men outside himself; they symbolized something that in his studious solitariness he was apt not to believe in. He could stand at Piccadilly Circus, could watch the crowds shuffle past, and still imagine himself the one fully conscious, intelligent, individual being among all those thousands. It seemed, somehow, impossible that other people should be in their way as elaborate and complete as he in his. Impossible; and yet, periodically he would make some painful discovery about the external world and the horrible reality of its consciousness and its intelligence. The red notebook was one of these discoveries, a footprint in the sand. It put beyond a doubt the fact that the outer world really existed.

Sitting on the balustrade of the terrace, he ruminated this unpleasant truth for some time. Still chewing on it, he strolled pensively down towards the swimming-pool. A peacock and his hen trailed their shabby finery across the turf of the lower lawn. Odious birds! Their necks, thick and greedily fleshy at the roots, tapered up to the cruel inanity of their brainless heads, their flat eyes and piercing beaks. The fabulists were right, he reflected, when they took beasts to illustrate their tractates of human morality. Animals resemble men with all the truthfulness of a caricature. (Oh, the red notebook!) He threw a piece of stick at the slowly pacing birds. They rushed towards it, thinking it was something to eat.

He walked on. The profound shade of a giant ilex tree engulfed him. Like a great wooden octopus, it spread its long arms abroad.

Under the spreading ilex tree . . .'

He tried to remember who the poem was by, but couldn't.

'The smith, a brawny man is he,
With arms like rubber bands.'

Just like his; he would have to try and do his Muller exercises more regularly.

He emerged once more into the sunshine. The pool lay before him, reflecting in its bronze mirror the blue and various green of the summer day. Looking at it, he thought of Anne's bare arms and seal-sleek bathing-dress, her moving knees and feet.

'And little Luce with the white legs,
And bouncing Barbary . . .'

Oh, these rags and tags of other people's making! Would

he ever be able to call his brain his own? Was there, indeed, anything in it that was truly his own, or was it simply an education?

He walked slowly round the water's edge. In an embayed recess among the surrounding yew trees, leaning her back against the pedestal of a pleasantly comic version of the Medici Venus, executed by some nameless mason of the *seicento*, he saw Mary pensively sitting.

'Hullo!' he said, for he was passing so close to her that he had to say something.

Mary looked up. 'Hullo!' she answered in a melancholy, uninterested tone.

In this alcove, hewed out of the dark trees, the atmosphere seemed to Denis agreeably elegiac. He sat down beside her under the shadow of the pubic goddess. There was a prolonged silence.

At breakfast that morning Mary had found on her plate a picture postcard of Gobley Great Park. A stately Georgian pile, with a façade sixteen windows wide; parterres in the foreground; huge, smooth lawns receding out of the picture to right and left. Ten years more of the hard times and Gobley, with all its peers, will be deserted and decaying. Fifty years, and the countryside will know the old landmarks no more. They will have vanished as the monasteries vanished before them. At the moment, however, Mary's mind was not moved by these considerations.

On the back of the postcard, next to the address, was written, in Ivor's bold, large hand, a single quatrain.

'Hail, maid of moonlight! Bride of the sun, farewell!
Like bright plumes moulted in an angel's flight,
There sleep within my heart's most mystic cell
Memories of morning, memories of the night.'

There followed a postscript of three lines: 'Would you mind asking one of the housemaids to forward the packet of safety-razor blades I left in the drawer of my washstand. Thanks. – IVOR.'

Seated under the Venus's immemorial gesture, Mary considered life and love. The abolition of her repressions, so far from bringing the expected peace of mind, had brought nothing but disquiet, a new and hitherto unexperienced

139

Ivor, Ivor. . . . She couldn't do without him now.
evident on the other hand, from the poem on the
the picture postcard, that Ivor could very well do
without her. He was at Gobley now; so was Zenobia. Mary
knew Zenobia. She thought of the last verse of the song he
had sung that night in the garden.

> 'Le lendemain, Phillis peu sage
> Aurait donné moutons et chien
> Pour un baiser que le volage
> A Lisette donnait pour rien.'

Mary shed tears at the memory; she had never been so
unhappy in all her life before.

It was Denis who first broke the silence. 'The individual,'
he began in a soft and sadly philosophical tone, 'is not a self-
supporting universe. There are times when he comes into
contact with other individuals, when he is forced to take
cognizance of the existence of other universes beside himself.'

He had contrived this highly abstract generalization as a
preliminary to a personal confidence. It was the first gambit
in a conversation that was to lead up to Jenny's caricatures.

'True,' said Mary; and, generalizing for herself, she added,
'When one individual comes into intimate contact with another, she – or he, of course, as the case may be – must almost
inevitably receive or inflict suffering.'

'One is apt,' Denis went on, 'to be so spellbound by the
spectacle of one's own personality that one forgets that the
spectacle presents itself to other people as well as to oneself.'

Mary was not listening. 'The difficulty,' she said, 'makes
itself acutely felt in matters of sex. If one individual seeks
intimate contact with another individual in the natural way,
she is certain to receive or inflict suffering. If, on the other
hand, she avoids contacts, she risks the equally grave sufferings that follow on unnatural repressions. As you see, it's a
dilemma.'

'When I think of my own case,' said Denis, making a more
decided move in the desired direction, 'I am amazed how
ignorant I am of other people's mentality in general and,
above all and in particular, of their opinions about myself.
Our minds are sealed books only occasionally opened to the

outside world.' He made a gesture that was faintly suggestive of the drawing off of a rubber band.

'It's an awful problem,' said Mary thoughtfully. 'One has to have had personal experience to realize quite how awful it is.'

'Exactly.' Denis nodded. 'One has to have had first-hand experience.' He leaned towards her and slightly lowered his voice. 'This very morning, for example . . .' he began, but his confidences were cut short. The deep voice of the gong, tempered by distance to a pleasant booming, floated down from the house. It was lunch-time. Mechanically Mary rose to her feet, and Denis, a little hurt that she should exhibit such a desperate anxiety for her food and so slight an interest in his spiritual experiences, followed her. They made their way up to the house without speaking.

CHAPTER XXV

'I hope you all realize,' said Henry Wimbush during dinner, 'that next Monday is Bank Holiday, and that you will all be expected to help in the Fair.'

'Heavens!' cried Anne. 'The Fair – I had forgotten all about it. What a nightmare! Couldn't you put a stop to it, Uncle Henry?'

Mr Wimbush sighed and shook his head. 'Alas,' he said, 'I fear I cannot. I should have liked to put an end to it years ago; but the claims of Charity are strong.'

'It's not charity we want,' Anne murmured rebelliously; 'it's justice.'

'Besides,' Mr Wimbush went on, 'the Fair has become an institution. Let me see, it must be twenty-two years since we started it. It was a modest affair then. Now . . .' he made a sweeping movement with his hand and was silent.

It spoke highly for Mr Wimbush's public spirit that he still continued to tolerate the Fair. Beginning as a sort of glorified church bazaar, Crome's yearly Charity Fair had grown into a noisy thing of merry-go-rounds, cocoa-nut shies, and miscellaneous side shows – a real genuine fair on the grand scale. It was the local St Bartholomew, and the people of all the neighbouring villages, with even a contingent from the county town, flocked into the park for their Bank Holiday amusement. The local hospital profited handsomely, and it was this fact alone which prevented Mr Wimbush, to whom the Fair was a cause of recurrent and never-diminishing agony, from putting a stop to the nuisance which yearly desecrated his park and garden.

'I've made all the arrangements already,' Henry Wimbush went on. 'Some of the larger marquees will be put up tomorrow. The swings and the merry-go-round arrive on Sunday.'

'So there's no escape,' said Anne, turning to the rest of the party. 'You'll all have to do something. As a special favour you're allowed to choose your slavery. My job is the tea tent, as usual, Aunt Priscilla . . .'

'My dear,' said Mrs Wimbush, interrupting her, 'I have more important things to think about than the Fair. But you need have no doubt that I shall do my best when Monday comes to encourage the villagers.'

'That's splendid,' said Anne. 'Aunt Priscilla will encourage the villagers. What will you do, Mary?'

'I won't do anything where I have to stand by and watch other people eat.'

'Then you'll look after the children's sports.'

'All right,' Mary agreed. 'I'll look after the children's sports.'

'And Mr Scogan?'

Mr Scogan reflected. 'May I be allowed to tell fortunes?' he asked at last. 'I think I should be good at telling fortunes.'

'But you can't tell fortunes in that costume!'

'Can't I?' Mr Scogan surveyed himself.

'You'll have to be dressed up. Do you still persist?'

'I'm ready to suffer all indignities.'

'Good!' said Anne; and turning to Gombauld, 'You must be our lightning artist,' she said. ' "Your portrait for a shilling in five minutes." '

'It's a pity I'm not Ivor,' said Gombauld, with a laugh. 'I could throw in a picture of their Auras for an extra sixpence.'

Mary flushed. 'Nothing is to be gained,' she said severely, 'by speaking with levity of serious subjects. And, after all, whatever your personal views may be, psychical research is a perfectly serious subject.'

'And what about Denis?'

Denis made a deprecating gesture. 'I have no accomplishments,' he said. 'I'll just be one of those men who wear a thing in their buttonholes and go about telling people which is the way to tea and not to walk on the grass.'

'No, no,' said Anne. 'That won't do. You must do something more than that.'

'But what? All the good jobs are taken, and I can do nothing but lisp in numbers.'

'Well, then, you must lisp,' concluded Anne. 'You must write a poem for the occasion – an "Ode on Bank Holiday." We'll print it on Uncle Henry's press and sell it at twopence a copy.'

'Sixpence,' Denis protested. 'It'll be worth sixpence.'

Anne shook her head. 'Twopence,' she repeated firmly. 'Nobody will pay more than twopence.'

'And now there's Jenny,' said Mr Wimbush. 'Jenny,' he said, raising his voice, 'what will you do?'

Denis thought of suggesting that she might draw caricatures at sixpence an execution, but decided it would be wiser to go on feigning ignorance of her talent. His mind reverted to the red notebook. Could it really be true that he looked like that?

'What will I do,' Jenny echoed, 'what will I do?' She frowned thoughtfully for a moment; then her face brightened and she smiled. 'When I was young,' she said, 'I learnt to play the drums.'

'The drums?'

Jenny nodded, and, in proof of her assertion, agitated her knife and fork, like a pair of drumsticks, over her plate. 'If there's any opportunity of playing the drums . . .' she began.

'But of course,' said Anne, 'there's any amount of opportunity. We'll put you down definitely for the drums. That's the lot,' she added.

'And a very good lot too,' said Gombauld. 'I look forward to my Bank Holiday. It ought to be gay.'

'It ought indeed,' Mr Scogan assented. 'But you may rest assured that it won't be. No holiday is ever anything but a disappointment.'

'Come, come,' protested Gombauld. 'My holiday at Crome isn't being a disappointment.'

'Isn't it?' Anne turned an ingenuous mask towards him.

'No, it isn't,' he answered.

'I'm delighted to hear it.'

'It's in the very nature of things,' Mr Scogan went on; 'our holidays can't help being disappointments. Reflect for a moment. What is a holiday? The ideal, the Platonic Holiday of Holidays is surely a complete and absolute change. You agree with me in my definition?' Mr Scogan glanced from face to face round the table; his sharp nose moved in a series of rapid jerks through all the points of the compass. There was no sign of dissent; he continued: 'A complete and absolute change; very well. But isn't a complete and absolute change precisely the thing we can never have – never, in the very nature of things?' Mr Scogan once more looked rapidly about him. 'Of course it is. As ourselves, as specimens of Homo Sapiens, as members of a society, how can we hope to have anything like an absolute change? We are tied down by the frightful limitation of our human faculties, by the notions which society imposes on us through our fatal suggestibility, by our own personalities. For us, a complete holiday is out of the question. Some of us struggle manfully to take one, but we never succeed, if I may be allowed to express myself metaphorically, we never succeed in getting farther than Southend.'

'You're depressing,' said Anne.

'I mean to be,' Mr Scogan replied, and, expanding the fingers of his right hand, he went on : 'Look at me, for example. What sort of a holiday can I take? In endowing me with passions and faculties Nature has been horribly niggardly. The full range of human potentialities is in any case distressingly limited; my range is a limitation within a limitation. Out of the ten octaves that make up the human instrument, I can compass perhaps two. Thus, while I may have a certain amount of intelligence, I have no aesthetic sense; while I possess the mathematical faculty, I am wholly without the religious emotions; while I am naturally addicted to venery, I have little ambition and am not at all avaricious. Education has further limited my scope. Having been brought up in society, I am impregnated with its laws; not only should I be afraid of taking a holiday from them, I should also feel it painful to try to do so. In a word, I have a conscience as well as a fear of gaol. Yes, I know it by experience. How often have I tried to take holidays, to get away from myself, my own boring nature, my insufferable mental surroundings !' Mr Scogan sighed. 'But always without success,' he added, 'always without success. In my youth I was always striving – how hard ! – to feel religiously and aesthetically. Here, said I to myself, are two tremendously important and exciting emotions. Life would be richer, warmer, brighter, altogether more amusing, if I could feel them. I tried to feel them. I read the works of the mystics. They seemed to me nothing but the most deplorable claptrap – as indeed they always must to anyone who does not feel the same emotion as the authors felt when they were writing. For it is the emotion that matters. The written work is simply an attempt to express emotion, which is in itself inexpressible, in terms of intellect and logic. The mystic objectifies a rich feeling in the pit of the stomach into a cosmology. For other mystics that cosmology is a symbol of the rich feeling. For the unreligious it is a symbol of nothing, and so appears merely grotesque. A melancholy fact! But I divagate.' Mr Scogan checked himself. 'So much for the religious emotion. As for the aesthetic – I was at even greater pains to cultivate that. I have looked at all the right works of art in every part of Europe. There was a time when, I venture to believe, I knew more about Taddeo da Poggibonsi, more about the cryptic Amico di Taddeo, even than Henry does. Today, I am happy to say, I have forgotten most of the knowledge I then so laboriously acquired; but without vanity I can assert that it was prodigious. I don't pretend, of course, to know anything about nigger sculpture or the later seventeenth century in Italy; but about all the periods that were fashionable before 1900 I am, or was, omniscient. Yes, I repeat it, omniscient. But did that fact make me any more appreciative of art in general? It did not. Confronted by a picture, of which I could tell you all the known and presumed history – the date when it was painted, the character of the painter, the influences that had gone to make it what it was – I felt none of that strange excitement and exaltation which is, as I am informed by those who do feel it, the true aesthetic emotion. I felt nothing but a certain interest in the subject of the picture; or more often, when the subject was hackneyed and religious, I felt nothing but a great weariness of spirit. Nevertheless, I must have gone on looking at pictures for ten years before I would honestly admit to myself that they merely bored me. Since then I have given up all attempts to take a holiday. I go on cultivating my old stale daily self in the resigned spirit with which a bank clerk performs from ten till six his daily task. A holiday, indeed! I'm sorry for you, Gombauld, if you still look forward to having a holiday.'

Gombauld shrugged his shoulders. 'Perhaps,' he said, 'my standards aren't as elevated as yours. But personally I found the war quite as thorough a holiday from all the ordinary decencies and sanities, all the common emotions and preoccupations, as I ever want to have.'

'Yes,' Mr Scogan thoughtfully agreed. 'Yes, the war was certainly something of a holiday. It was a step beyond Southend; it was Weston-super-Mare; it was almost Ilfracombe.'

CHAPTER XXVI

A little canvas village of tents and booths had sprung up, just beyond the boundaries of the garden, in the green expanse of the park. A crowd thronged its streets, the men dressed mostly in black – holiday best, funeral best – the women in pale muslins. Here and there tricolour bunting hung inert. In the midst of the canvas town, scarlet and gold and crystal, the merry-go-round glittered in the sun. The balloon-man walked among the crowd, and above his head, like a huge, inverted bunch of many-coloured grapes, the balloons strained upwards. With a scythe-like motion the boat-swings reaped the air, and from the funnel of the engine which worked the roundabout rose a thin, scarcely wavering column of black smoke.

Denis had climbed to the top of one of Sir Ferdinando's towers, and there, standing on the sun-baked leads, his elbows resting on the parapet, he surveyed the scene. The steam-organ sent up prodigious music. The clashing of automatic cymbals beat out with inexorable precision the rhythm of piercingly sounded melodies. The harmonies were like a musical shattering of glass and brass. Far down in the bass the Last Trump was hugely blowing, and with such persistence, such resonance, that its alternate tonic and dominant detached themselves from the rest of the music and made a tune of their own, a loud, monotonous see-saw.

Denis leaned over the gulf of swirling noise. If he threw himself over the parapet, the noise would surely buoy him up, keep him suspended, bobbing, as a fountain balances a ball on its breaking crest. Another fancy came to him, this time in metrical form.

'My soul is a thin white sheet of parchment stretched
  Over a bubbling cauldron.'

Bad, bad. But he liked the idea of something thin and distended being blown up from underneath.

'My soul is a thin tent of gut. . . .'

148

or better –

'My soul is a pale, tenuous membrane. . . .'

That was pleasing : a thin, tenuous membrane. It had the right anatomical quality. Tight blown, quivering in the blast of noisy life. It was time for him to descend from the serene empyrean of words into the actual vortex. He went down slowly. 'My soul is a thin, tenuous membrane. . . .'

On the terrace stood a knot of distinguished visitors. There was old Lord Moleyn, like a caricature of an English milord in a French comic paper : a long man, with a long nose and long, drooping moustaches and long teeth of old ivory, and lower down, absurdly, a short covert coat, and below that long, long legs cased in pearl-grey trousers – legs that bent unsteadily at the knee and gave a kind of sideways wobble as he walked. Beside him, short and thick-set, stood Mr Callamay, the venerable, conservative statesman, with a face like a Roman bust, and short white hair. Young girls didn't much like going for motor drives alone with Mr Callamay; and of old Lord Moleyn one wondered why he wasn't living in gilded exile on the island of Capri among the other distinguished persons who, for one reason or another, find it impossible to live in England. They were talking to Anne, laughing, the one profoundly, the other hootingly.

A black silk balloon towing a black-and-white striped parachute proved to be old Mrs Budge from the big house on the other side of the valley. She stood low on the ground, and the spikes of her black-and-white sunshade menaced the eyes of Priscilla Wimbush, who towered over her – a massive figure dressed in purple and topped with a queenly toque on which the nodding black plumes recalled the splendours of a first-class Parisian funeral.

Denis peeped at them discreetly from the window of the morning-room. His eyes were suddenly become innocent, childlike, unprejudiced. They seemed, these people, inconceivably fantastic. And yet they really existed, they functioned by themselves, they were conscious, they had minds. Moreover, he was like them. Could one believe it? But the evidence of the red notebook was conclusive.

It would have been polite to go and say, 'How d'you do?' But at the moment Denis did not want to talk, could not have talked. His soul was a tenuous, tremulous, pale membrane. He would keep its sensibility intact and virgin as long as he could. Cautiously he crept out by a side door and made his way down towards the park. His soul fluttered as he approached the noise and movement of the fair. He paused for a moment on the brink, then stepped in and was engulfed.

Hundreds of people, each with his own private face and all of them real, separate, alive : the thought was disquieting. He paid twopence and saw the Tattooed Woman; twopence more, the Largest Rat in the World. From the home of the Rat he emerged just in time to see a hydrogen-filled balloon break loose for home. A child howled up after it; but calmly, a perfect sphere of flushed opal, it mounted, mounted. Denis followed it with his eyes until it became lost on the blinding sunlight. If he could but send his soul to follow it ! . . .

He sighed, stuck his steward's rosette in his buttonhole, and started to push his way, aimlessly but officially, through the crowd.

CHAPTER XXVII

Mr Scogan had been accommodated in a little canvas hut.
Dressed in a black shirt and a red bodice, with a yellow-and-
red bandana handkerchief tied round his black wig, he
looked – sharp-nosed, brown, and wrinkled – like the Bohemian hag of Frith's Derby Day. A placard pinned to the
curtain of the doorway announced the presence within the
tent of 'Sesostris, the Sorceress of Ecbatana.' Seated at a
table, Mr Scogan received his clients in mysterious silence,
indicating with a movement of the finger that they were to
sit down opposite him and to extend their hands for his
inspection. He then examined the palm that was presented
him, using a magnifying glass and a pair of horn spectacles.
He had a terrifying way of shaking his head, frowning and
clicking with his tongue as he looked at the lines. Sometimes he would whisper, as though to himself, 'Terrible, terrible !' or 'God preserve us !' sketching out the sign of the
cross as he uttered the words. The clients who came in laughing grew suddenly grave; they began to take the witch
seriously. She was a formidable-looking woman; could it be,
was it possible, that there was something in this sort of thing
after all? After all, they thought, as the hag shook her head
over their hands, after all . . . And they waited, with an uncomfortably beating heart, for the oracle to speak. After a
long and silent inspection, Mr Scogan would suddenly look
up and ask, in a hoarse whisper, some horrifying question,
such as, 'Have you ever been hit on the head with a hammer
by a young man with red hair?' When the answer was in
the negative, which it could hardly fail to be, Mr Scogan
would nod several times, saying, 'I was afraid so. Everything is still to come, still to come, though it can't be very far
off now.' Sometimes, after a long examination, he would
just whisper, 'Where ignorance is bliss, 'tis folly to be wise,'
and refuse to divulge any details of a future too appalling to
be envisaged without despair. Sesostris had a success of horror. People stood in a queue outside the witch's booth waiting
for the privilege of hearing sentence pronounced upon them.

Denis, in the course of his round, looked with curiosity at this crowd of suppliants before the shrine of the oracle. He had a great desire to see how Mr Scogan played his part. The canvas booth was a rickety, ill-made structure. Between its walls and its sagging roof were long gaping chinks and crannies. Denis went to the tea-tent and borrowed a wooden bench and a small Union Jack. With these he hurried back to the booth of Sesostris. Setting down the bench at the back of the booth, he climbed up, and with a great air of busy efficiency began to tie the Union Jack to the top of one of the tent-poles. Through the crannies in the canvas he could see almost the whole of the interior of the tent. Mr Scogan's bandana-covered head was just below him; his terrifying whispers came clearly up. Denis looked and listened while the witch prophesied financial losses, death by apoplexy, destruction by air-raids in the next war.

'Is there going to be another war?' asked the old lady to whom he had predicted this end.

'Very soon,' said Mr Scogan, with an air of quiet confidence.

The old lady was succeeded by a girl dressed in white muslin, garnished with pink ribbons. She was wearing a broad hat, so that Denis could not see her face; but from her figure and the roundness of her bare arms he judged her young and pleasing. Mr Scogan looked at her hand then, whispered, 'You are still virtuous.'

The young lady giggled and exclaimed, 'Oh, lor'!'

'But you will not remain so for long,' added Mr Scogan sepulchrally. The young lady giggled again. 'Destiny, which interests itself in small things no less than in great, has announced the fact upon your hand.' Mr Scogan took up the magnifying-glass and began once more to examine the white palm. 'Very interesting,' he said, as though to himself – 'very interesting. It's as clear as day.' He was silent.

'What's clear?' asked the girl.

'I don't think I ought to tell you.' Mr Scogan shook his head; the pendulous brass ear-rings which he had screwed on to his ears tinkled.

'Please, please !' she implored.

The witch seemed to ignore her remark. 'Afterwards, it's not at all clear. The fates don't say whether you will settle down to married life and have four children or whether you will try to go on the cinema and have none. They are only specific about this one rather crucial incident.'

'What is it? What is it? Oh, do tell me!'

The white muslin figure leant eagerly forward.

Mr Scogan sighed. 'Very well,' he said, 'if you must know, you must know. But if anything untoward happens you must blame your own curiosity. Listen. Listen.' He lifted up a sharp, claw-nailed forefinger. 'This is what the fates have written. Next Sunday afternoon at six o'clock you will be sitting on the second stile on the footpath that leads from the church to the lower road. At that moment a man will appear walking along the footpath.' Mr Scogan looked at her hand again as though to refresh his memory of the details of the scene. 'A man,' he repeated – 'a small man with a sharp nose, not exactly good looking nor precisely young, but fascinating.' He lingered hissingly over the word. 'He will ask you, "Can you tell me the way to Paradise?" and you will answer, "Yes, I'll show you," and walk with him down towards the little hazel copse. I cannot read what will happen after that.' There was a silence.

'Is it really true?' asked white muslin.

The witch gave a shrug of the shoulders. 'I merely tell you what I read in your hand. Good afternoon. That will be sixpence. Yes, I have change. Thank you. Good afternoon.'

Denis stepped down from the bench; tied insecurely and crookedly to the tent-pole, the Union Jack hung limp on the windless air. 'If only I could do things like that!' he thought, as he carried the bench back to the tea-tent.

Anne was sitting behind a long table filling thick white cups from an urn. A neat pile of printed sheets lay before her on the table. Denis took one of them and looked at it affectionately. It was his poem. They had printed five hundred copies, and very nice the quarto broad-sheets looked.

'Have you sold many?' he asked in a casual tone.

Anne put her head on one side deprecatingly. 'Only three so far, I'm afraid. But I'm giving a free copy to everyone who spends more than a shilling on his tea. So in any case it's having a circulation.'

Denis made no reply, but walked slowly away. He looked

at the broadsheet in his hand and read the lines to himself
relishingly as he walked along :

> 'This day of roundabouts and swings,
> Struck weights, shied cocoa-nuts, tossed rings,
> Switchbacks, Aunt Sallies, and all such small
> High jinks – you call it ferial?
> A holiday? But paper noses
> Sniffed the artificial roses
> Of round Venetian cheeks through half
> Each carnival year, and masks might laugh
> At things the naked face for shame
> Would blush at – laugh and think no blame.
> A holiday? But Galba showed
> Elephants on an airy road;
> Jumbo trod the tightrope then,
> And in the circus armèd men
> Stabbed home for sport and died to break
> Those dull imperatives that make
> A prison of every working day,
> Where all must drudge and all obey.
> Sing Holiday! You do not know
> How to be free. The Russian snow
> Flowered with bright blood whose roses spread
> Petals of fading, fading red
> That died into the snow again,
> Into the virgin snow; and men
> From all the ancient bonds were freed
> Old law, old custom, and old creed,
> Old right and wrong there bled to death :
> The frozen air received their breath,
> A little smoke that died away;
> And round about them where they lay
> The snow bloomed roses. Blood was there
> A red-gay flower and only fair.
> Sing Holiday! Beneath the Tree
> Of Innocence and Liberty,
> Paper Nose and Red Cockade
> Dance within the magic shade
> That makes them drunken, merry, and strong
> To laugh and sing their ferial song :

"Free, free . . . !"
               But Echo answers
Faintly to the laughing dancers,
"Free" – and faintly laughs, and still,
Within the hollows of the hill,
Faintlier laughs and whispers, "Free,"
Fadingly, diminishingly :
"Free," and laughter faints away . . .
Sing Holiday ! Sing Holiday !'

He folded the sheet carefully and put it in his pocket. The thing has its merits. Oh, decidedly, decidedly ! But how unpleasant the crowd smelt ! He lit a cigarette. The smell of cows was preferable. He passed through the gate in the park wall into the garden. The swimming-pool was a centre of noise and activity.

'Second Heat in the Young Ladies' Championship.' It was the polite voice of Henry Wimbush. A crowd of sleek, seal-like figures in black bathing-dresses surrounded him. His grey bowler hat, smooth, round, and motionless in the midst of a moving sea, was an island of aristocratic calm.

Holding his tortoise-shell-rimmed pince-nez an inch or two in front of his eyes, he read out names from a list.

'Miss Dolly Miles, Miss Rebecca Balister, Miss Doris Gabell . . .'

Five young persons ranged themselves on the brink. From their seats of honour at the other end of the pool, old Lord Moleyn and Mr Callamay looked on with eager interest.

Henry Wimbush raised his hand. There was an expectant silence. 'When I say "Go," go. Go !' he said. There was an almost simultaneous splash.

Denis pushed his way through the spectators. Somebody plucked him by the sleeve; he looked down. It was old Mrs Budge.

'Delighted to see you again, Mr Stone,' she said in her rich, husky voice. She panted a little as she spoke, like a short-winded lap-dog. It was Mrs Budge who, having read in the *Daily Mirror* that the Government needed peach stones – what they needed them for she never knew – had made the collection of peach stones her peculiar 'bit' of war work. She had thirty-six peach trees in her walled garden, as well as four hot-houses in which trees could be forced, so that she was able to eat peaches practically the whole year round. In 1916 she ate 4200 peaches, and sent the stones to the Government. In 1917 the military authorities called up three of her gardeners, and what with this and the fact that it was a bad year for wall fruit, she only managed to eat 2900 peaches during that crucial period of the national destinies. In 1918 she did rather better, for between January 1st and the date of the Armistice she ate 3300 peaches. Since the Armistice she had relaxed her efforts; now she did not eat more than two or three peaches a day. Her constitution, she complained, had suffered; but it had suffered for a good cause.

Denis answered her greeting by a vague and polite noise.

'So nice to see the young people enjoying themselves,' Mrs Budge went on. 'And the old people too, for that matter. Look at old Lord Moleyn and dear Mr Callamay. Isn't it delightful to see the way they enjoy themselves?'

Denis looked. He wasn't sure whether it was so very delightful after all. Why didn't they go and watch the sack races? The two old gentlemen were engaged at the moment in congratulating the winner of the race; it seemed an act of supererogatory graciousness; for, after all, she had only won a heat.

'Pretty little thing, isn't she?' said Mrs Budge huskily, and panted two or three times.

'Yes,' Denis nodded agreement. Sixteen, slender, but nubile, he said to himself, and laid up the phrase in his memory as a happy one. Old Mr Callamay had put on his spectacles to congratulate the victor, and Lord Moleyn, leaning forward over his walking-stick, showed his long ivory teeth, hungrily smiling.

'Capital performance, capital,' Mr Callamay was saying in his deep voice.

The victor wriggled with embarrassment. She stood with her hands behind her back, rubbing one foot nervously on the other. Her wet bathing-dress shone, a torso of black polished marble.

'Very good indeed,' said Lord Moleyn. His voice seemed to come from just behind his teeth, a toothy voice. It was as though a dog should suddenly begin to speak. He smiled again, Mr Callamay readjusted his spectacles.

'When I say "Go," go. Go!'

Splash! The third heat had started.

'Do you know, I never could learn to swim,' said Mrs Budge.

'Really?'

'But I used to be able to float.'

Denis imagined her floating – up and down, up and down on a great green swell. A blown black bladder; no, that wasn't good, that wasn't good at all. A new winner was being congratulated. She was atrociously stubby and fat. The last one, long and harmoniously, continuously curved from knee to breast, had been an Eve by Cranach; but this, this one was a bad Rugens.

'. . . go – go – go!' Henry Wimbush's polite level voice once more pronounced the formula. Another batch of young ladies dived in.

Grown a little weary of sustaining a conversation with Mrs Budge, Denis conveniently remembered that his duties as a steward called him elsewhere. He pushed out through the lines of spectators and made his way along the path left clear behind them. He was thinking again that his soul was a pale, tenuous membrane, when he was startled by hearing a thin, sibilant voice, speaking apparently from just above his head, pronounce the single word 'Disgusting!'

He looked up sharply. The path along which he was walking passed under the lee of a wall of clipped yew. Behind the hedge the ground sloped steeply up towards the foot of the terrace and the house; for one standing on the higher ground it was easy to look over the dark barrier. Looking up, Denis saw two heads overtopping the hedge immediately above him. He recognized the iron mask of Mr Bodiham and the pale, colourless face of his wife. They were looking over his head, over the heads of the spectators, at the swimmers in the pond.

'Disgusting!' Mrs Bodiham repeated, hissing softly.

The rector turned up his iron mask towards the solid cobalt of the sky. 'How long?' he said, as though to himself; 'how long?' He lowered his eyes again, and they fell on Denis's upturned curious face. There was an abrupt movement, and Mr and Mrs Bodiham popped out of sight behind the hedge.

Denis continued his promenade. He wandered past the merry-go-round, through the thronged streets of the canvas village; the membrane of his soul flapped tumultuously in the noise and laughter. In a roped-off space beyond, Mary was directing the children's sports. Little creatures seethed round about her, making a shrill, tiny clamour; others clustered about the skirts and trousers of their parents. Mary's face was shining in the heat; with an immense output of energy she started a three-legged race. Denis looked on in admiration.

'You're wonderful,' he said, coming up behind her and touching her on the arm.

'I've never seen such energy.'

She turned towards him a face, round, red, and honest as the setting sun; the golden bell of her hair swung silently as she moved her head and quivered to rest.

'Do you know, Denis,' she said, in a low, serious voice, gasping a little as she spoke – 'do you know that there's a woman here who has had three children in thirty-one months?'

'Really,' said Denis, making rapid mental calculations.

'It's appalling. I've been telling her about the Malthusian League. One really ought . . .'

But a sudden violent renewal of the metallic yelling announced the fact that somebody had won the race. Mary became once more the centre of a dangerous vortex. It was time, Denis thought, to move on; he might be asked to do something if he stayed too long.

He turned back towards the canvas village. The thought of tea was making itself insistent in his mind. Tea, tea, tea. But the tea-tent was horribly thronged. Anne, with an unusual expression of grimness on her flushed face, was furiously working the handle of the urn; the brown liquid spurted incessantly into the proffered cups. Portentous, in the farther corner of the tent, Priscilla, in her royal toque, was encouraging the villagers. In a momentary lull Denis could hear her deep, jovial laughter and her manly voice. Clearly, he told himself, this was no place for one who wanted tea. He stood irresolute at the entrance to the tent. A beautiful thought suddenly came to him : if he went back to the house, went unobtrusively, without being observed, if he tip-toed into the dining-room and noiselessly opened the little doors of the side-board – ah, then ! In the cool recess within he would find bottles and a siphon; a bottle of crystal gin and a quart of soda water, and then for the cups that inebriate as well as cheer. . . .

A minute later he was walking briskly up the shady yew-tree walk. Within the house it was deliciously quiet and cool. Carrying his well-filled tumbler with care, he went into the library. There, the glass on the corner of the table beside him, he settled into a chair with a volume of Sainte-Beuve. There was nothing, he found, like a Causerie du Lundi for settling and soothing the troubled spirits. That tenuous membrane of his had been too rudely buffeted by the afternoon's emotions; it required a rest.

CHAPTER XXVIII

Towards sunset the fair itself became quiescent. It was the
hour for the dancing to begin. At one side of the village of
tents a space had been roped off. Acetylene lamps, hung
round it on posts, cast a piercing white light. In one corner
sat the band, and, obedient to its scraping and blowing, two
or three hundred dancers trampled across the dry ground,
wearing away the grass with their booted feet. Round this
patch of all but daylight, alive with motion and noise, the
night seemed preternaturally dark. Bars of light reached out
into it, and every now and then a lonely figure or a couple
of lovers, interlaced, would cross the bright shaft, flashing
for a moment into visible existence, to disappear again as
quickly and surprisingly as they had come.

Denis stood by the entrance of the enclosure, watching
the swaying, shuffling crowd. The slow vortex brought the
couples round and round again before him, as though he
were passing them in review. There was Priscilla, still wearing her queenly toque, still encouraging the villagers – this
time by dancing with one of the tenant farmers. There was
Lord Moleyn, who had stayed on to the disorganized, pass-
overish meal that took the place of dinner of this festal day;
he one-stepped shamblingly, his bent knees more precariously
wobbly than ever, with a terrified village beauty. Mr Scogan
trotted round with another. Mary was in the embrace of a
young farmer of heroic proportions; she was looking up at
him, talking, as Denis could see, very seriously. What about?
he wondered. The Malthusian League, perhaps. Seated in
the corner among the band, Jenny was performing wonders
of virtuosity upon the drums. Her eyes shone, she smiled to
herself. A whole subterranean life seemed to be expressing
itself in those loud rat-tats, those long rolls and flourishes of
drumming. Looking at her, Denis ruefully remembered the
red notebook; he wondered what sort of a figure he was
cutting now. But the sight of Anne and Gombauld swimming
past – Anne with her eyes almost shut and sleeping, as it
were, on the sustaining wings of movement and music –

dissipated these preoccupations. Male and female created He them. . . . There they were, Anne and Gombauld, and a hundred couples more – all stepping harmoniously together to the old tune of Male and Female created He them. But Denis sat apart; he alone lacked his complementary opposite. They were all coupled but he; all but he. . . .

Somebody touched him on the shoulder and he looked up. It was Henry Wimbush.

'I never showed you our oaken drain-pipes,' he said. 'Some of the ones we dug up are lying quite close to here. Would you like to come and see them?'

Denis got up, and they walked off together into the darkness. The music grew fainter behind them. Some of the higher notes faded out altogether. Jenny's drumming and the steady sawing of the bass throbbed on, tuneless and meaningless in their ears. Henry Wimbush halted.

'Here we are,' he said, and, taking an electric torch out of his pocket, he cast a dim beam over two or three blackened sections of tree trunk, scooped out into the semblance of pipes, which were lying forlornly in a little depression in the ground.

'Very interesting,' said Denis, with a rather tepid enthusiasm.

They sat down on the grass. A faint white glare, rising from behind a belt of trees, indicated the position of the dancing-floor. The music was nothing but a muffled rhythmic pulse.

'I shall be glad,' said Henry Wimbush, 'when this function comes at last to an end.'

'I can believe it.'

'I do not know how it is,' Mr Wimbush continued, 'but the spectacle of numbers of my fellow-creatures in a state of agitation moves in me a certain weariness, rather than any gaiety or excitement. That fact is, they don't very much interest me. They aren't in my line. You follow me? I could never take much interest, for example, in a collection of postage stamps. Primitives or seventeenth-century books – yes. They are my line. But stamps, no. I don't know anything about them; they're not my line. They don't interest me, they give me no emotion. It's rather the same with people, I'm afraid. I'm more at home with these pipes.' He jerked his head sideways towards the hollowed logs. 'The trouble with the people and events of the present is that you never know anything about them. What do I know of contemporary politics? Nothing. What do I know of the people I see round about me? Nothing. What they think of me or of anything else in the world, what they will do in five minutes' time, are things I can't guess at. For all I know, you may suddenly jump up and try to murder me in a moment's time.'

'Come, come,' said Denis.

'True,' Mr Wimbush continued, 'the little I know about your past is certainly reassuring. But I know nothing of your present, and neither you nor I know anything of your future. It's appalling; in living people, one is dealing with unknown and unknowable quantities. One can only hope to find out anything about them by a long series of the most disagreeable and boring human contacts, involving a terrible expense of time. It's the same with current events; how can I find out anything about them except by devoting years to the most exhausting first-hand study, involving once more an endless number of the most unpleasant contacts? No, give me the past. It doesn't change; it's all there in black and white, and you can get to know about it comfortably and decorously and, above all, privately – by reading. By reading I know a great deal of Caesar Borgia, of St Francis, of Dr Johnson; a few weeks have made me thoroughly acquainted with these interesting characters, and I have been spared the tedious and revolting process of getting to know them by personal contact, which I should have to do if they were living now. How gay and delightful life would be if one could get rid of all the human contacts! Perhaps, in the future, when machines have attained to a state of perfection – for I confess that I am, like Godwin and Shelley, a believer in perfectibility, the perfectibility of machinery – then, perhaps, it will be possible for those who, like myself, desire it, to live in a dignified seclusion, surrounded by the delicate attentions of silent and graceful machines, and entirely secure from any human intrusion. It is a beautiful thought.'

'Beautiful,' Denis agreed. 'But what about the desirable human contacts, like love and friendship?'

The black silhouette against the darkness shook its head.

'The pleasures even of these contacts are much [over]ted,' said the polite level voice. 'It seems to m[e]whether they are equal to the pleasures of priv[ate?]and contemplation. Human contacts have bee[n]valued in the past only because reading was not a common accomplishment and because books were scarce and difficult to reproduce. The world, you must remember, is only just becoming literate. As reading becomes more and more habitual and widespread, an ever-increasing number of people will discover that books will give them all the pleasures of social life and none of its intolerable tedium. At present people in search of pleasure naturally tend to congregate in large herds and to make a noise; in future their natural tendency will be to seek solitude and quiet. The proper study of mankind is books.'

'I sometimes think that it may be,' said Denis; he was wondering if Anne and Gombauld were still dancing together.

'Instead of which,' said Mr Wimbush, with a sigh, 'I must go and see if all is well on the dancing-floor.' They got up and began to walk slowly towards the white glare. 'If all these people were dead,' Henry Wimbush went on, 'this festivity would be extremely agreeable. Nothing would be pleasanter than to read in a well-written book of an open-air ball that took place a century ago. How charming! one would say; how pretty and how amusing! But when the ball takes place today, when one finds oneself involved in it, then one sees the thing in its true light. It turns out to be merely this.' He waved his hand in the direction of the acetylene flares. 'In my youth,' he went on after a pause, 'I found myself, quite fortuitously, involved in a series of the most phantasmagorical amorous intrigues. A novelist could have made his fortune out of them, and even if I were to tell you, in my bald style, the details of these adventures, you would be amazed at the romantic tale. But I assure you, while they were happening – these romantic adventures – they seemed to me no more and no less exciting than any other incident of actual life. To climb by night up a rope-ladder to a second-floor window in an old house in Toledo seemed to me, while I was actually performing this rather dangerous feat, an action as obvious, as much to be taken for granted, as

163

how shall I put it? – as quotidian as catching the 8.52 from Surbiton to go to business on a Monday morning. Adventures and romance only take on their 'adventurous and romantic qualities at second-hand. Live them, and they are just a slice of life like the rest. In literature they become as charming as this dismal ball would be if we were celebrating its tercentenary.' They had come to the entrance of the enclosure and stood there, blinking in the dazzling light. 'Ah, if only we were!' Henry Wimbush added.

Anne and Gombauld were still dancing together.

CHAPTER XXIX

It was after ten o'clock. The dancers had already dispersed and the last lights were being put out. Tomorrow the tents would be struck, the dismantled merry-go-round would be packed into waggons and carted away. An expanse of worn grass, a shabby brown patch in the wide green of the park, would be all that remained. Crome Fair was over.

By the edge of the pool two figures lingered.

'No, no, no,' Anne was saying in a breathless whisper, leaning backwards, turning her head from side to side in an effort to escape Gombauld's kisses. 'No, please. No.' Her raised voice had become imperative.

Gombauld relaxed his embrace a little. 'Why not?' he said. 'I will.'

With a sudden effort Anne freed herself. 'You won't,' she retorted. 'You've tried to take the most unfair advantage of me.'

'Unfair advantage?' echoed Gombauld in genuine surprise.

'Yes, unfair advantage. You attack me after I've been dancing for two hours, while I'm still reeling drunk with the movement, when I've lost my head, when I've got no mind left but only a rhythmical body! It's as bad as making love to someone you've drugged or intoxicated.'

Gombauld laughed angrily. 'Call me a White Slaver and have done with it.'

'Luckily,' said Anne, 'I am now completely sobered, and if you try and kiss me again I shall box your ears. Shall we take a few turns round the pool?' she added. 'The night is delicious.'

For answer Gombauld made an irritated noise. They paced off slowly, side by side.

'What I like about the painting of Degas . . .' Anne began in her most detached and conversational tone.

'Oh, damn Degas!' Gombauld was almost shouting.

From where he stood, leaning in an attitude of despair against the parapet of the terrace, Denis had seen them, the two pale figures in a patch of moonlight, far down by the pool's edge. He had seen the beginning of what promised to be an endlessly passionate embracement, and at the sight he had fled. It was too much; he couldn't stand it. In another moment, he felt, he would have burst into irrepressible tears.

Dashing blindly into the house, he almost ran into Mr Scogan, who was walking up and down the hall smoking a final pipe.

'Hullo!' said Mr Scogan, catching him by the arm; dazed and hardly conscious of what he was doing or where he was, Denis stood there for a moment like a somnambulist. 'What's the matter?' Mr Scogan went on. 'You look disturbed, distressed, depressed.'

Denis shook his head without replying.

'Worried about the cosmos, eh?' Mr Scogan patted him on the arm. 'I know the feeling,' he said. 'It's a most distressing symptom. "What's the point of it all? All is vanity. What's the good of continuing to function if one's doomed to be snuffed out at last along with everything else?" Yes, yes. I know exactly how you feel. It's most distressing if one allows oneself to be distressed. But then why allow oneself to be distressed? After all, we all know that there's no ultimate point. But what difference does that make?'

At this point the somnambulist suddenly woke up. 'What?' he said, blinking and frowning at his interlocutor. 'What?' Then breaking away he dashed up the stairs, two steps at a time.

Mr Scogan ran to the foot of the stairs and called up after him. 'It makes no difference, none whatever. Life is gay all the same, always, under whatever circumstances – under whatever circumstances,' he added, raising his voice to a shout. But Denis was already far out of hearing, and even if he had not been, his mind tonight was proof against all the consolations of philosophy. Mr Scogan replaced his pipe between his teeth and resumed his meditative pacing. 'Under any circumstances,' he repeated to himself. It was ungrammatical to begin with; was it true? And is life really its own reward? He wondered. When his pipe had burned itself to its stinking conclusion he took a drink of gin and went to bed. In ten minutes he was deeply, innocently asleep.

Denis had mechanically undressed and, clad in those flowered silk pyjamas of which he was so justly proud, was lying face downwards on his bed. Time passed. When at last he looked up, the candle which he had left alight at his bedside had burned down almost to the socket. He looked at his watch; it was nearly half-past one. His head ached, his dry, sleepless eyes felt as though they had been bruised from behind, and the blood was beating within his ears a loud arterial drum. He got up, opened the door, tiptoed noiselessly along the passage, and began to mount the stairs towards the higher floors. Arrived at the servants' quarters under the roof, he hesitated, then turning to the right he opened a little door at the end of the corridor. Within was a pitch-dark cupboard-like boxroom, hot, stuffy, and smelling of dust and old leather. He advanced cautiously into the blackness, groping with his hands. It was from this den that the ladder went up to the leads of the western tower. He found the ladder, and set his feet on the rungs; noiselessly, he lifted the trapdoor above his head; the moonlit sky was over him, he breathed the fresh, cool air of the night. In a moment he was standing on the leads, gazing out over the dim, colourless landscape, looking perpendicularly down at the terrace seventy feet below.

Why had he climbed up to this high, desolate place? Was it to look at the moon? Was it to commit suicide? As yet he hardly knew. Death – the tears came into his eyes when he thought of it. His misery assumed a certain solemnity; he was lifted up on the wings of a kind of exaltation. It was a mood in which he might have done almost anything, however foolish. He advanced towards the farther parapet; the drop was sheer there and uninterrupted. A good leap, and perhaps one might clear the narrow terrace and so crash down yet another thirty feet to the sun-baked ground below. He paused at the corner of the tower, looking now down into the shadowy gulf below, now up towards the rare stars and the waning moon. He made a gesture with his hand, muttered something, he could not afterwards remember what; but the fact that he had said it aloud gave the utterance a peculiarly terrible significance. Then he looked down once more into the depths.

'What *are* you doing, Denis?' questioned a voice from somewhere very close behind him.

Denis uttered a cry of frightened surprise, and very nearly went over the parapet in good earnest. His heart was beating terribly, and he was pale when, recovering himself, he turned round in the direction from which the voice had come.

'Are you ill?'

In the profound shadow that slept under the eastern parapet of the tower, he saw something he had not previously noticed – an oblong shape. It was a mattress, and someone was lying on it. Since that first memorable night on the tower, Mary had slept out every evening; it was a sort of manifestation of fidelity.

'It gave me a fright,' she went on, 'to wake up and see you waving your arms and gibbering there. What on earth were you doing?'

Denis laughed melodramatically. 'What, indeed !' he said. If she hadn't woken up as she did, he would be lying in pieces at the bottom of the tower; he was certain of that, now.

'You hadn't got designs on me, I hope?' Mary inquired, jumping too rapidly to conclusions.

'I didn't know you were here,' said Denis, laughing more bitterly and artificially than before.

'What *is* the matter, Denis?'

He sat down on the edge of the mattress, and for all reply went on laughing in the same frightful and improbable tone.

An hour later he was reposing with his head on Mary's knees, and she, with an affectionate solicitude that was wholly maternal, was running her fingers through his tangled hair. He had told her everything, everything : his hopeless love, his jealousy, his despair, his suicide – as it were providentially averted by her interposition. He had solemnly promised never to think of self-destruction again. And now his soul was floating in a sad serenity. It was embalmed in the sympathy that Mary so generously poured. And it was not only in receiving sympathy that Denis found serenity and even a kind of happiness; it was also in giving it. For if he had told Mary everything about his miseries, Mary, reacting to these confidences, had told him in return everything, or very nearly everything, about her own.

'Poor Mary!' He was very sorry for her. Still, she might have guessed that Ivor wasn't precisely a monument of constancy.

'Well,' she concluded, 'one must put a good face on it.' She wanted to cry, but she wouldn't allow herself to be weak. There was a silence.

'Do you think,' asked Denis hesitatingly – 'do you really think that she ... that Gombauld ...'

'I'm sure of it,' Mary answered decisively. There was another long pause.

'I don't know what to do about it,' he said at last, utterly dejected.

'You'd better go away,' advised Mary. 'It's the safest thing, and the most sensible.'

'But I've arranged to stay here three weeks more.'

'You must concoct an excuse.'

'I suppose you're right.'

'I know I am,' said Mary, who was recovering all her firm self-possession. 'You can't go on like this, can you?'

'No, I can't go on like this,' he echoed.

Immensely practical, Mary invented a plan of action. Startlingly, in the darkness, the church clock struck three.

'You must go to bed at once,' she said. 'I'd no idea it was so late.'

Denis clambered down the ladder, cautiously descended the creaking stairs. His room was dark; the candle had long ago guttered to extinction. He got into bed and fell asleep almost at once.

CHAPTER XXX

Denis had been called, but in spite of the parted curtains he had dropped off again into that drowsy, dozy state when sleep becomes a sensual pleasure almost consciously savoured. In this condition he might have remained for another hour if he had not been disturbed by a violent rapping at the door.

'Come in,' he mumbled, without opening his eyes. The latch clicked, a hand seized him by the shoulder and he was rudely shaken.

'Get up, get up!'

His eyelids blinked painfully apart, and he saw Mary standing over him, bright-faced and earnest.

'Get up!' she repeated. 'You must go and send the telegram. Don't you remember?'

'O Lord!' He threw off the bed-clothes; his tormentor retired.

Denis dressed as quickly as he could and ran up the road to the village post office. Satisfaction glowed within him as he returned. He had sent a long telegram, which would in a few hours evoke an answer ordering him back to town at once – on urgent business. It was an act performed, a decisive step taken – and he so rarely took decisive steps; he felt pleased with himself. It was with a whetted appetite that he came in to breakfast.

'Good morning,' said Mr Scogan. 'I hope you're better.'

'Better?'

'You were rather worried about the cosmos last night.'

Denis tried to laugh away the impeachment. 'Was I?' he lightly asked.

'I wish,' said Mr Scogan, 'that I had nothing worse to prey on my mind. I should be a happy man.'

'One is only happy in action,' Denis enunciated, thinking of the telegram.

He looked out of the window. Great florid baroque clouds floated high in the blue heaven. A wind stirred among the trees, and their shaken foliage twinkled and glittered like metal in the sun. Everything seemed marvellously beautiful. At the thought that he would soon be leaving all this beauty he felt a momentary pang; but he comforted himself by recollecting how decisively he was acting.

'Action,' he repeated aloud, and going over to the sideboard he helped himself to an agreeable mixture of bacon and fish.

Breakfast over, Denis repaired to the terrace, and sitting there, raised the enormous bulwark of *The Times* against the possible assaults of Mr Scogan, who showed an unappeased desire to go on talking about the Universe. Secure behind the crackling pages, he meditated. In the light of this brilliant morning the emotions of last night seemed somehow rather remote. And what if he had seen them embracing in the moonlight? Perhaps it didn't mean much after all. And even if it did, why shouldn't he stay? He felt strong enough to stay, strong enough to be aloof, disinterested, a mere friendly acquaintance. And even if he weren't strong enough . . .

'What time do you think the telegram will arrive?' asked Mary suddenly, thrusting in upon him over the top of the paper.

Denis started guiltily. 'I don't know at all,' he said.

'I was only wondering,' said Mary, 'because there's a very good train at 3.27, and it would be nice if you could catch it, wouldn't it?'

'Awfully nice,' he agreed weakly. He felt as though he were making arrangements for his own funeral. Train leaves Waterloo 3.27. No flowers. . . . Mary was gone. No, he was blowed if he'd let himself be hurried down to the Necropolis like this. He was blowed. The sight of Mr Scogan looking out, with a hungry expression, from the drawing-room window made him precipitately hoist *The Times* once more. For a long while he kept it hoisted. Lowering it at last to take another cautious peep at his surroundings, he found himself, with what astonishment! confronted by Anne's faint, amused, malicious smile. She was standing before him, – the woman who was a tree, – the swaying grace of her movement arrested in a pose that seemed itself a movement.

'How long have you been standing there?' he asked, when he had done gaping at her.

'Oh, about half an hour, I suppose,' she said airily. 'You were so very deep in your paper – head over ears – I didn't like to disturb you.'

'You look lovely this morning,' Denis exclaimed. It was the first time he had ever had the courage to utter a personal remark of the kind.

Anne held up her hand as though to ward off a blow. 'Don't bludgeon me, please.' She sat down on the bench beside him. He was a nice boy, she thought, quite charming; and Gombauld's violent insistences were really becoming rather tiresome. 'Why don't you wear white trousers?' she asked. 'I like you so much in white trousers.'

'They're at the wash,' Denis replied rather curtly. This white-trouser business was all in the wrong spirit. He was just preparing a scheme to manoeuvre the conversation back to the proper path, when Mr Scogan suddenly darted out of the house, crossed the terrace with clockwork rapidity, and came to a halt in front of the bench on which they were seated.

'To go on with our interesting conversation about the cosmos,' he began. 'I become more and more convinced that the various parts of the concern are fundamentally discrete. . . . But would you mind, Denis, moving a shade to your right?' He wedged himself between them on the bench. 'And if you would shift a few inches to the left, my dear Anne. . . . Thank you. Discrete, I think, was what I was saying.'

'You were,' said Anne. Denis was speechless.

They were taking their after-luncheon coffee in the library when the telegram arrived. Denis blushed guiltily as he took the orange envelope from the salver and tore it open. 'Return at once. Urgent family business.' It was too ridiculous. As if he had any family business! Wouldn't it be best just to crumple the thing up and put it in his pocket without saying anything about it? He looked up; Mary's large blue china eyes were fixed upon him, seriously, penetratingly. He blushed more deeply than ever, hesitated in a horrible uncertainty.

'What's your telegram about?' Mary asked significantly. He lost his head. 'I'm afraid,' he mumbled, 'I'm afraid this means I shall have to go back to town at once.' He frowned at the telegram ferociously.

'But that's absurd, impossible,' cried Anne. She had been standing by the window talking to Gombauld; but at Denis's words she came swaying across the room towards him.

'It's urgent,' he repeated desperately.

'But you've only been here such a short time,' Anne protested.

'I know,' he said, utterly miserable. Oh, if only she could understand! Women were supposed to have intuition.

'If he must go, he must,' put in Mary firmly.

'Yes, I must.' He looked at the telegram again for inspiration. 'You see, it's urgent family business,' he explained.

Priscilla got up from her chair in some excitement. 'I had a distinct presentiment of this last night,' she said. 'A distinct presentiment.'

'A mere coincidence, no doubt,' said Mary, brushing Mrs Wimbush out of the conversation. 'There's a very good train at 3.27.' She looked at the clock on the mantelpiece. 'You'll have nice time to pack.'

'I'll order the motor at once.' Henry Wimbush rang the bell. The funeral was well under way. It was awful, awful.

'I'm wretched you should be going,' said Anne.

Denis turned towards her; she really did look wretched. He abandoned himself hopelessly, fatalistically to his destiny. This was what came of action, of doing something decisive. If only he'd just let things drift! If only . . .

'I shall miss your conversation,' said Mr Scogan.

Mary looked at the clock again. 'I think perhaps you ought to go and pack,' she said.

Obediently Denis left the room. Never again, he said to himself, never again would he do anything decisive. Camlet, West Bowlby, Knipswich for Timpany, Spavin Delawarr; and then all the other stations; and then, finally, London. The thought of the journey appalled him. And what on earth was he going to do in London when he got there? He climbed wearily up the stairs. It was time for him to lay himself in his coffin.

The car was at the door – the hearse. The whole party had assembled to see him go. Good-bye, good-bye. Mechanically he tapped the barometer that hung in the porch; the needle stirred perceptibly to the left. A sudden smile lighted up his lugubrious face.

' "It stinks, and I am ready to depart," ' he said, quoting Landor with an exquisite aptness. He looked quickly round from face to face. Nobody had noticed. He climbed into the hearse.

THE WORLD'S GREATEST NOVELISTS NOW AVAILABLE IN TRIAD/GRANADA PAPERBACKS

Aldous Huxley

Brave New World	£1.25 ☐
Island	£1.95 ☐
After Many a Summer	£1.95 ☐
Brief Candles	£1.50 ☐
The Doors of Perception/	
Heaven and Hell	£1.50 ☐
The Devils of Loudun	£1.95 ☐
Eyeless in Gaza	£1.95 ☐
Antic Hay	£1.95 ☐
Crome Yellow	95p ☐
Point Counter Point	£1.95 ☐
Those Barren Leaves	£1.95 ☐
The Human Situation (non-fiction)	£1.50 ☐

Hermann Hesse

Stories of Five Decades	£1.95 ☐
Journey to the East	£1.25 ☐
Demian	£1.25 ☐
My Belief (non-fiction)	£1.25 ☐
Reflections (non-fiction)	95p ☐
Hermann Hesse: A Pictorial Biography	£1.50 ☐

All these books are available at your local bookshop or newsagent, or can be ordered direct from the publisher. Just tick the titles you want and fill in the form below.

Name _____

Address _____

_____

Write to Granada Cash Sales
PO Box 11, Falmouth, Cornwall TR10 9EN.

Please enclose remittance to the value of the cover price plus:

UK 45p for the first book, 20p for the second book plus 14p per copy for each additional book ordered to a maximum charge of £1.63.

BFPO and Eire 45p for the first book, 20p for the second book plus 14p per copy for the next 7 books, thereafter 8p per book.

Overseas 75p for the first book and 21p for each additional book.

Granada Publishing reserve the right to show new retail prices on covers, which may differ from those previously advertised in the text or elsewhere.